The Adventure Begins!

Lorrie climbed on the rocking horse and he began to rock, faster and faster—

There was a wind blowing and leaves whirled up—leaves? Lorrie blinked. This was not the dollhouse room, it was a road with trees on either side and the wind in their branches. She was not on a rocking horse at all, but on a real one. And she wore a long skirt flapping in the wind. For a moment she was stiff with fright, and then that fright vanished. Dimly she had a strange feeling she had done this before, that this was just as it should be.

The white horse moved easily at a steady trot, and Lorrie rode him as if this was the most natural thing in the world. Not too far ahead was a brick house. The Octagon House! Lorrie's heart beat faster. Something, someone was waiting there for her and it was most important. . . .

Octagon Magic

Andre Norton

AN ARCHWAY PAPERBACK
POCKET BOOKS . NEW YORK

*For my mother, whose beloved
stories of a late Victorian
childhood made those years very real
for me. And for Viola, Ernestine,
and Becky, who made suggestions.*

 POCKET BOOKS, a Simon & Schuster division of
GULF & WESTERN CORPORATION
1230 Avenue of the Americas, New York, N.Y. 10020

Published by arrangement with The World Publishing Company
Library of Congress Catalog Card Number: 67-13822

ISBN: 0-671-56074-3

First Pocket Books printing October, 1978

10 9 8 7 6 5 4 3 2

Trademarks registered in the United States and other countries.

Printed in the U.S.A.

Contents

Witch's House

"CANUCK, Canuck, walks like a duck!"

Lorrie Mallard walked a little faster, staring straight ahead. She was determined not to run, but she could not shut out those hateful words. Two blocks yet to go, with Jimmy Purvis and Stan Wormiski and Rob Lockner all close behind.

"Canuck——"

There was a prickle in her nose, but she was not going to cry—she was not! And neither was she going to run so they could chase her all the way to the apartment house. Boys—mean, hateful boys! Staring and laughing and whispering about you in class, trying to pull your hair or trip you up or grab your book bag in the halls, trailing you home singing that mean, hateful song. Two blocks more . . .

1

Unless she took the short cut by the witch's house.

Lorrie turned her head, just enough to sight the beginning of the alley, the one where the tangle of overgrown brush hung in a big choked mass over the rusty iron of the old fence. It looked just like the jungle pictures in the social studies book, if the jungle had lost all its leaves in a storm.

Social studies! Lorrie frowned. Back home in Canada at Miss Logan's School they did not have social studies, any more than they had boys. They had *history* and she had done well in history. But now it seemed she had learned the wrong kind of history. She did not belong. If only Grandmother had not had to go off to England where her old friend could care for her after her operation.

"Canuck—"

Lorrie turned into the alley. You could see the top of the witch's house above all the trees and bushes. Was it just a big old garden filled up with trees and plants growing wild, Lorrie wondered. There was a gate opening onto the alley, but it had a chain across it as rusty as the iron fence. No one had opened that for a long, long time, she guessed. Of course, a witch wouldn't need a gate anyway. She could just fly over on her broom.

"Canuck—"

Lorrie gripped her book bag tighter. Her small pointed chin rose a fraction of an inch, her lips set stubbornly. A possible witch behind a locked gate was not nearly so bad as Jimmy, Stan, and Rob. Now she deliberately slowed down.

The boys and the girls were afraid, or said they were, of the witch's house. Lorrie had heard them daring one another to climb the fence, to rap at the front door. Not that anyone, even Jimmy Purvis, had ever done it.

On her right, on the opposite side of the alley, was a red-brick building with the glass all broken out of the windows, and boards nailed across them. It had once been a stable where horses and carriages were kept. Then came the end of the parking lot for the apartment house where Lorrie lived, all cold and bare with only a couple of cars in it at this time of the afternoon.

Wind swept up the alley. Leaves spun and rustled along with it. Most of the trees and bushes behind the fence were bare. Still one could not see in very far, the branches and trunks were so thick.

Lorrie did not really believe that a witch lived there, or that there was a ghost groaning inside either, even though Kathy Lockner swore it was so. Aunt Margaret had said it was just an old, old house unlike any built today. Octagon House they called it because it had really eight sides. And there was an old lady living there who could not walk very well, so she never came out.

Swinging her book bag to the other hand, Lorrie went up to the chained gate. The house

3

was queer, what she could see of it. Now, greatly daring, she squeezed her arm between the bars of the gate, leaving streaks of rust on her windbreaker, and pushed aside two branches to clear the view. Yes, it was very different. She could see steps and a door, and an angled wall with very tall, pointed windows. Lorrie made up her mind.

She would take part of that dare, even though they had never made it to her. She was going to walk all around the witch house, see all of it that she could. Setting down her bag, she tried to brush off some of the rust marks. This was the end of the alley and she turned north on Ash Street, instead of south, walking slowly along the front of the house.

Here the brush-and-tree jungle was not as high or as thick as by the alley. There was an opening and Lorrie halted with a little gasp of surprise. The last time she had come this way she had been hurrying to keep up with Aunt Margaret, who always seemed to be a step or two ahead. That had been just after she had come to Ashton when there had still been leaves on all the branches, so she had not seen the deer, as big as a real one, but black and green—not brown— as if moss grew on him.

Lorrie pushed closer to the fence. The deer stood on a big stone block, and there was a brick wall, all the bricks laid crooked with green moss between them. Then came the house. It had tall windows—the ones she could see had shutters across them—and a door. Leaves had drifted high all over, as if no one ever swept them up to be burned.

Lorrie bit down on her lower lip. . . . Burning leaves in big heaps, the smoke that smelled so good. Once, they had put three big potatoes right in the middle of the fire. Those became all black on the outside, but you broke them open and ate them with a little salt. And the squirrels had come up and asked for bits.

She had been only a little girl then. Why, that must have been five—six years ago. But she could remember it, though now she did not want to. Not when she lived here where there were no leaves to burn, nothing—where they called her a stupid, silly Canuck—though she did *not* walk like a duck!

Lorrie set her bag on the ground between her two feet so she could hold the bars of the front gate. There was no chain, but of course it was locked. All those leaves . . .

There was a big oak tree in the yard at Miss Logan's. You hunted for acorns and tried to find the biggest one. She never had, but Anne, her best friend did last year, a whopper—almost as big as Lorrie's thumb. Miss Logan's—Anne—Lorrie fought the nose-prickling sensation again.

Everything had gone wrong for her here in Ashton. Maybe if she had arrived when school started and not come late when everyone had already made friends and she was alone— No, she was different anyway, she was a stupid Canuck, wasn't she?

Her troubles had started the day of the big test last month. There had been a substitute teacher—Mrs. Raymond had had the flu. And she had been so cross when Lorrie had not understood the questions. Could Lorrie help it if she came from Canada where they had taught different things? She had always had high grades in Miss Logan's School and Grandmother Mallard had been proud of her. She had never asked to come to Ashton and live with Aunt Margaret Gerson, who was away working all day, when Grandmother had had to go for her operation. All the things they taught at Miss Logan's seemed wrong here. When she had answered the first time in class, said, "Yes, Mrs. Raymond," and curtsied, they had all laughed, every one of them. All those hateful boys bobbing up and down in the yard afterward and yelling, "Yes, ma-am, no, ma'am." There had been no boys at Miss Logan's —hateful things!

And she could not talk about the same things that Kathy and the rest of the girls did. Now Mrs. Raymond mentioned putting her back a grade, saying she was too slow in catching up. Put back—just because they had different lessons here.

Then Jimmy Purvis made up that song, and they all sang at her on the way home. She did not like to go home when Aunt Margaret was gone, and Mrs. Lockner kept saying she must come over to their apartment and not stay alone.

Lorrie blinked hard several times. The deer had looked watery and wavery, but now he was sturdy and strong again. She wished she could see him closer. There was a big leaf caught on the prong of one of his antlers and it flapped up and down like a little flag. Lorrie smiled. There was something funny about that. The deer was so big and proud, and kind of stern, but that leaf flip-flapped as if making fun of him.

In spite of the shuttered windows, all the dark trees and bushes and the big piles of leaves, Lorrie liked this house. It was not a scary place at all.

Or were there two kinds of witches? The mean, scary kind was one, and then there were those like the Princess' grandmother in *The Princess and Curdie*. A fairy godmother had magic powers. Only she made good things, instead of bad, happen. She could use a fairy godmother now, one to transform Jimmy Purvis into a *real* duck.

Lorrie grinned as she picked up her book bag. Old Jimmy Purvis with yellow feathers all over him and big flat feet—that was the first thing she would ask for if a fairy godmother, or a good witch, said she could have some wishes. She had better get home now. She could say she had homework to do so Mrs. Lockner would leave her alone in Aunt Margaret's apartment.

On impulse Lorrie lifted her hand in salute to the deer. The wind gave an extra tug at that moment and tore the leaf flag from his antler, soaring it over the gate to Lorrie's feet. She pounced upon it, torn as it was, and tucked it into the pocket of her windbreaker. Why, she did not know.

Then she turned south toward the apartment. She had just reached the mouth of the alley when she heard a thin cry. Something in that sound halted her.

"It went in there! Poke it, Stan, poke it out here and I'll catch it!"

Jimmy Purvis knelt by a bush growing near the old stable. Stan Wormiski, his lieutenant and faithful follower, thrust a long branch into a tangle of weeds, while Rob Lockner stood by. Stan and Jimmy were excited, but Rob looked a little unhappy.

"Go on, Stan, poke!" Jimmy ordered. "Get it out. I'll grab it!"

Again that thin, unhappy cry. Lorrie found herself running, not away from the gang this time, but toward them. Just before she reached the boys, a small black shadow burst from the weeds, dodged past Jimmy, and sprang at her.

Needle-pointed claws cut through her tights, then grabbed her skirt, and her windbreaker, as a frenzied kitten swarmed up Lorrie as if she were a tree. She threw her arm protectingly around it and faced the boys.

"Well, look who's here. Old dummy Canuck. That's a witch cat, Canuck, give it to me. Give it here, now!" Jimmy came at her, grinning.

"No!" Lorrie swung her book bag as a defensive barrier. Against her chest, under her other hand, the kitten was a shivering mass of fur, still crying with tiny shrieks of fear.

"Give it here, Canuck." Jimmy was still grinning, but Lorrie was frightened. He did not look in the least as if he meant this for fun, not the kind of fun she recognized.

She turned and ran, away from that look in Jimmy's eyes. She could not gain the apartment before they caught up with her, of that she was sure. And if she did, with Aunt Margaret gone, who would take her side?

Maybe—maybe she could get over the fence, hide in the bushes. She used to climb a lot—in that yard of bonfires and happy times. There was the front gate, and the fancy curves in it ought to make good holds. Lorrie threw her book bag up and over, pushed the now feebly struggling kitten into the front of her windbreaker, and began to climb with a speed born of desperation.

Why the boys had not already caught up with her, she did not know. Maybe Jimmy Purvis would not dare follow her in here. But she wasted no time in looking around to see. Lorrie topped the gate, swung over and down, landing in an awkward tumble on the crazy pattern of the brick wall.

The kitten fought furiously for freedom, leaped to the path, and scuttled on among the leaves, heading around the house rather than to the front door. That, to Lorrie, looked as if it were never opened. Afraid that in its fright it might dash back to the alley again, she scrambled up to follow.

She saw the bright red of Jimmy's windbreaker, the soiled gray of Stan's. They were coming along the outside of the fence on Ash Street, but not very fast. Suppose they followed her in here?

Lorrie's retreat was as fast as the kitten's as she followed in its wake. It was several moments before she realized that, for all the piles of leaves through which she rustled, this was relatively clear ground. There was a walk of the crisscross brick going around the side of the house, and it was bordered by beds where stood stalks crowned by the withered heads of frost-killed flowers. The heavy growth of bushes and trees was only along the fence, screening this inner part.

She glanced at the house as she rounded one of its angles. The windows here were not covered by shutters, but the shades were drawn so she could not see in.

"Merroww—" That was the kitten. Lorrie hurried on.

Rounding another angle she came to a place where the bordering flower beds of the walk widened out into squares. These were bare, as if whatever had grown there had been carefully harvested. More of the tall thin windows, but these were neither shuttered nor shaded. She saw the white of a curtain and an edge of dark red drape at one. If the front of the house had been closed, it was not so here.

Lorrie stopped running, and walked slowly and almost warily along the path. Leaves were here, too, blowing and gathering in heaps. In the center of the cleared beds was an empty pool. Centering that was a crouching thing, a dragon, Lorrie thought. It held its head high at a rather uncomfortable angle, with a small black pipe just showing in its wide open mouth, as if it had once spit water—instead of the fire storybook dragons blew at their knightly enemies—into the basin at its clawed feet.

"Merrow!" The kitten's voice pulled her on, around another angle. Here was the door she had seen from the chained gate. On one of the steps beneath it crouched the kitten, its mouth open to emit another small but piercing wail.

Lorrie stiffened at a creaking louder than the kitten's cry. She stopped short, to watch the door. It was opening, and as soon as a big enough crack showed, the kitten whisked through. But the door continued to open and Lorrie discovered she could not have run, not even if she had wanted to, for her feet seemed as firmly fixed as if she had stepped into a roadway surfaced with sticky tar.

It was dark inside the house. Though on this

late fall afternoon lights had already appeared in the windows elsewhere on the street, none showed here. But the woman who stood in the doorway was perfectly visible to Lorrie.

She was small, hardly much taller than Lorrie herself, and her shoulders were rounded, making her bend forward. Her face had a large, broad nose and a chin that pushed up and forward in an effort to meet it. Above her dark brown cheeks and forehead, her black-and-gray hair crisply curled together, what showed of it, for she wore a cap with a frilled edge that made a stiff frame all around her head. Her dress was of a deep, dark red, and the skirt was very long and full under a large white apron that had a starched ruffle on the lower hem. With her hand on the latch of the door, the woman stood on the top step looking down at Lorrie. Then she smiled, and the droop of her nose, the sharp upturn of her chin, were forgotten.

"Hullo, little missy." Her voice was very soft and low. "How, you, Sabina, where's you bin, an' what's you bin doin'—gittin' all frazed up this heah way?"

From beneath the edge of her skirt popped the kitten's black head. Its round blue eyes surveyed the woman for a long instant and then turned to stare unblinkingly at Lorrie.

"Some boys," began Lorrie hurriedly, "they—"

The head in the frilled cap was already nodding. "They was up to tricks, aye, tricks. But you saw Sabina came to no harm, didn't you, little missy? I'll tell Mis' Charlotta, she'll be mighty pleased. You come in. Have a ginger cooky?"

Lorrie shook her head. "No, thank you. It's late. Mrs. Lockner—she'll tell Aunt Margaret I was late getting home. That would worry her."

"Come again then." The capped head bobbed, the smile grew even wider. "Now, how did you git in, little missy?"

"I climbed the gate, the front one," Lorrie admitted.

"An' did all that to your nice clothes. My, my." A brown finger pointed.

Lorrie looked down at herself. There were streaks of rust on the sleeves and the front of her windbreaker, more on her skirt and tights. She tried to brush off the worst of the stains.

"Come along. Hallie'll let you out, all right an' proper."

Down the steps she came, slowly and stiffly, as Lorrie waited. Then Lorrie followed that wide skirt as it brushed up leaves around the corners of the house, back to the front where the iron deer held his head high and proud. Hallie put her old, wrinkled hands on the gate, touched the top bar, and gave it a quick jerk. There was a small, protesting squeak and it moved inward, not all the way, for it stuck on the uneven bricks of the walk, but enough to let Lorrie through.

"Thank you." The manners that Miss Logan's classes had so carefully drilled came to Lorrie.

13

She ducked a small curtsy. "Thank you very much."

To her surprise Hallie's hand went to each side of the billowing skirt at which the wind was tugging, and the old woman made a stately, dipping acknowledgment that was far more graceful than any such gesture Lorrie had ever seen.

"You is welcome, little mis', entirely welcome."

Curiosity broke through good manners. "Are you—are you the—?"

Hallie's smile grew wider. "The ol' witch?" Her soft voice made that name sound worse.

Lorrie blushed. Not that she had ever been one of those who ran past Octagon House calling that name out, daring someone to go in and bang on the old witch's front door.

"The—the lady who lives here?" she stammered.

"I live heah, aye. But I'm Hallie, not Mis' Charlotta. Mis' Charlotta, she's Mis' Ashemeade."

Hallie made it sound, Lorrie thought, as if Miss Ashemeade was as grand a person as Lady Cartwright, a friend of Grandmother's in England.

And now Hallie's smile was gone and she sounded almost sharp. "Mis' Ashemeade, she's a great lady—don't you ever forget that."

"I—I won't. And I'm Lorrie Mallard." Lorrie held out her hand. "Very pleased to meet you."

Her fingers were enfolded in Hallie's. "An' I to meet you, Lorrie. Come again."

Lorrie trotted on down Ash Street. At the mouth of the alley she turned to glance back. But the gate was now firmly closed and Hallie was gone. What small scrap of house she could still see looked deserted.

It was colder and the wind blew stronger, pulling at her plaid skirt and cap. And the sky was dark, too, as if a storm were coming. Lorrie broke into a run, but she kept a sharp lookout. It would be just like Jimmy or Stan to hide out and pounce at her. She breathed a little easier as she skirted the parking lot. There were more cars there now, but none of them close enough to shelter lurking boys.

She clattered up the steps into the lobby of the apartment house. Mr. Parkinson was there, taking his mail out of the box. Lorrie slowed down and tried to close the door very quietly. Mr. Parkinson did not like children and he made that widely and forcibly known. There had been one afternoon when Kathy Lockner had thrown a ball all the way down the stairs and Lorrie picked it up, only to be accused of wild behavior, with threats of taking the matter to Aunt Margaret. She had avoided Mr. Parkinson carefully ever since.

He frowned at her now. Lorrie was very conscious of her rust-streaked clothing. And what would Aunt Margaret say if the marks did not come off? Clothes cost a lot of money, Lorrie knew that. Maybe if she brushed very hard—

But if Mr. Parkinson made his opinion of dirty and untidy little girls very plain in his stare, he did not put it into words. Lorrie edged past him and climbed the stairs as slowly and sedately as she could. But as soon as she hoped she was out of his sight, she hurried, her book bag bumping first against the stairs and then the walls as she went. Then she was at their own door, breathing fast, hunting under her jacket for the key. The Lockner door across the hall was closed. Mrs. Lockner was not watching for her.

Lorrie turned the key and slipped inside, shutting the door quickly behind her. Now she fronted the big mirror on the coat closet door and she gasped. No wonder Mr. Parkinson had stared so at her. She looked more of a mess than she had feared.

She hurried on to the bedroom she shared with her aunt. Then she pulled off her clothes, spreading them on her bed while she put on an old cotton dress. With a brush she set to work, trying to erase the marks left by her adventure.

Lucky, oh, she was lucky! Most of them brushed off. And those left were not too visible, even when she held them right under the lamp. This was Friday, too, so she could have another go at them in the morning. Finally she hung them up in the closet and went to the dressing table where all Aunt Margaret's nice-smelling bottles and jars were set out in a line against the base of the big mirror.

Such nice smells. There were lots of good smells in the world—burning leaves was one. Lorrie stood still, looking into the mirror, not now seeing her reflection but a picture out of memory. . . .

Mother and Daddy raking leaves for Lorrie to pack into a big basket. . . . Lorrie shook her head. She did not want to remember that because then she had to remember the rest. Mother and Daddy and the airplane that had taken them away from her forever. . . .

Lorrie closed her eyes and was determined not to remember. Now—she looked at the mirror

again—there was her face, rather like the cat heads she used to draw when she was little—a triangle. Her black hair was straying out of its ribbon tieback as it always did at this hour of the day. Lorrie set about remedying that with the same will and force she had given to brushing her clothes.

Greeny eyes—just like a cat's. Now suppose she did have a fairy godmother, what would be her next wish, after making Jimmy Purvis a big yellow duck? Yellow hair and blue eyes like Kathy Lockner's? No, Lorrie decided, she did not want those. What she had suited her well enough. She made the worst face she could think of at the mirror and laughed.

She smoothed down her skirt. What would it feel like, she wondered, to wear yards of skirt the way Hallie did? People all did in the olden days whether they were grown up or just girls. Lorrie enjoyed leafing through Aunt Margaret's costume books to look at the pictures. Aunt Margaret wrote advertising copy for Fredericka's Modes and knew all about high fashion. But nobody wore such dresses any more, so why did Hallie? Did she have only very old, old clothes? But the red dress had not looked old or worn. Or did Hallie wear just what she wanted to, and did not care if it were stylish to have a skirt short, or long, or in the middle?

Lorrie went on into the kitchen and began to bring packages out of the freezer section of the refrigerator. As she set the table in the dinette she thought of Jimmy and his gang. Jimmy would not forget her, but tomorrow was Saturday and then there was Sunday, no school, no Jimmy. So she had two days before she had to worry about him again.

If Aunt Margaret did not have to work overtime they would go shopping together in the morning. Then Lorrie could stop at the library. If only Aunt Margaret would stop worrying about why Lorrie did not have any close friends. Who needed the kinds of friends one could find about here? Kathy Lockner with all her silly jokes, and whispering about boys and playing those screechy records?

It was getting harder and harder to evade Aunt Margaret's pushing. Lorrie laid a napkin straight. She was not going to tell her that she did not like Kathy, or Kathy's friends.

There were some girls at school Lorrie would like to know better. Lizabeth Ross, for example. Lizabeth did not go around much with others, either. But she was smart and she liked to read the same sort of books. Lorrie had seen a copy of *The Secret Garden* on her desk. She had wanted to ask Lizabeth what part she liked best, and if she had read *A Little Princess* too. But then at recess Mrs. Raymond had kept Lorrie in for a talk about math mistakes and she had never had the chance. And Lizabeth lived down by Bruxten Drive and had never said anything to Lorrie except "hi." But to spend good time listening to Kathy's stupid old records, fussing with curlers in her hair, and talking silly—no!

Grandmother had never worried about her. If she just wanted to sit and read, that was fine. And she had had the right sort of friend in Anne. Only that was all gone, along with Miss Logan's, and what seemed now to Lorrie all peace and contentment. It was easy to forget the shadows and remember just sunny days when one wanted to.

Think of something else now—quick! Not Miss Logan's, or Hampstead, or Canada, or burning leaves or—Mother and Daddy—

The Octagon House, Lorrie seized upon that. The queer house, and the black kitten—Sabina, Hallie had called her—and Hallie herself. Hallie had asked her to come back. Maybe if she got out of school fast, and ran a lot of the way, she could some day.

Lorrie sat on the dinette bench and thought about it. There was nothing scary about the house she had seen. Was it strange inside, she wondered. What were the rooms like—three-cornered as wedges of pie? She would like to find out.

There was the click of a key in the hall door. Lorrie hurried through the rooms. Should she tell Aunt Margaret about her adventure, or part of it? Perhaps, but not yet, she decided just as the door opened.

The Bad Week and
Old Miss Ashemeade

THE BAD WEEK began early on Saturday with a blustery wind and a lot of clouds, plus the fact that Aunt Margaret's alarm clock failed to go off. She had extra work at the shop, and now she was so late she had no time for a proper breakfast, only the cup of coffee Lorrie poured for her while she scribbled down her grocery list.

There would be no shared shopping trip today. Aunt Margaret must try to get all the things they needed on her way home.

"Sorry, Chick." She frowned into the mirror of the closet as she put on her coat. "With the Christmas rush coming up, I can't get out of going to work today. But Mrs. Lockner will be driving to the shopping center and she'll let you visit the library. You just ask. Now"—she gave a swift glance around—"I think I have everything. Goodbye, Chick, and be good. Ohh, darn that clock anyway! I'm hours behind."

She was out and running down the hall, her heels click-clicking on the stairs, before Lorrie had more than time to blink. Slowly she went back to the kitchen and sat down to eat her cereal as she reviewed the ruins of all her plans. Outside the window, the dark clouds were already letting down spatters of rain and it looked thoroughly dismal.

Lorrie drank the rest of her orange juice. She was not going to say anything to Mrs. Lockner. A library visit with the Lockner clan was the last thing she wanted. Kathy and Rob had cards, or had had them. But they thought of the library as only another part of school where one was forced to go when the teacher said such and such a book had to be read. She had gone with them once and even now felt warm inside with remembered shame. Rob had been sent out for loud talking, and the librarian had warned Kathy and Lorrie, too, since Kathy had been talking to her. Kathy and Rob had both followed her around the shelves demanding what did she want *that* silly old book for, and saying every moment or so, "Come on! Hurry up, let's get going!"

To Lorrie a library must be enjoyed in peace and quiet, with plenty of time in which to choose a book. It took time to choose properly, since one was allowed to draw only two books at a time, and Lorrie was a fast reader. Most books lasted barely past Sunday afternoon, so size as well as subject matter was highly important. Only recently had she stumbled on pure treasure, a whole shelf of bound magazines, one year's issues all in one big heavy volume. They were old magazines, older than Aunt Margaret (though she had read some of them, too, when she was a little girl, because she had opened one and found a story she remembered), perhaps even older than Grandmother Mallard. But the stories in them were good.

Lorrie took her bowl, glass, and Anut Margaret's cup and saucer to the sink, and washed and dried them.

Her books were due and she wanted one at least of those *St. Nicholas* magazines. One would be all she could carry if she went alone, because that was just what she was going to do. It was easy when you planned it. She could go down to the corner of Wilton and Ash and take the Woodsville bus. That let you off at the shopping center. There was a stop light there so it was safe to cross the street to the library. Then, on the other side, was the bus stop to use coming home. But fare was twelve cents for children and she had a quarter.

Lorrie had never been to the library by herself, but there was no reason she could see why she could not go. Aunt Margaret had never said not to. Of course, Lorrie had never asked her about it, but she decided to ignore that thought.

It was raining harder. She would have to wear her raincoat and boots, and she would wrap up her books in a plastic bag. Lorrie moved briskly, putting the dishes away, mopping up the drain board and sink with a paper towel. The library did not open until ten, and it would take at least a half-hour to go. She had better leave a little after nine, or Mrs. Lockner might come over.

Lorrie sighed. People who wanted to be kind and helpful could certainly complicate life. "Kind and helpful," were Aunt Margaret's words for Mrs. Lockner. But to Lorrie, at times it seemed far more like interfering.

Now that she had made up her mind, she was excited. Why, she could do this every Saturday, and it would not matter how long she stayed at the library. No one would hurry her through her book selection, and she could even sit and read awhile. The thought of such bliss made Lorrie move restlessly from room to room, wishing the hand to go faster around the dial of the clock.

She was all dressed and ready at nine, hovering by the door with a nervous eye on the Lockner apartment across the hall. Then, unable to wait any longer, her books in their covering bag held tight against her, Lorrie locked the apartment and scuttled down the hall, though she took the steps at a slower pace.

It was raining really hard by the time she

reached the bus stop. But there was a shelter there and she stood waiting for what seemed hours before the bus appeared. Lorrie was pleased with her own resourcefulness when she got off at the shopping center.

There was another wait by the library door. She hunched over her books, hoping none of the wet would reach them, and her coat was damp across the shoulders when the guard opened the building at last.

Once inside, Lorrie forgot all but the delights she always enjoyed. She had all the time in the world to browse along the shelves, pulling out old favorites to read a sentence here and there, even though she knew the stories almost by heart. Time meant nothing until she became aware of a hollow feeling in her middle and glanced up at the room clock. Twelve o'clock! Surely that was as wrong as the alarm had been earlier.

Lorrie picked up the heavy, bound-magazine volume and with it her other choice, which she had read twice before, *Half Magic*, and hurried out to the charging desk.

"This is heavy to carry, isn't it?" asked the lady at the desk.

Lorrie shook her head determinedly. "I take the bus, I won't have far to carry it. Here"—She pulled the plastic cover from her pocket; she had wiped it off with her handkerchief and it did not seem too damp—"I can put this over them. They won't get wet."

"You won't need that, the rain is over. But I'm glad to see you know the proper way to take care of books."

Why shouldn't she, wondered Lorrie. People always seemed to think you didn't know about such things, and were surprised when you did. But maybe they were right to worry. She had seen Jimmy Purvis throw a book, actually throw it. And, when Stan had not caught it, it had hit the wall, to fall with loose pages. And Sally Walters had drawn pictures on the page margins in one of hers.

The rain might be over but the wind was cold. There was no bus shelter here, and she was so afraid of missing the next bus that she had to stand out by the sign on the curb where the wind swooped.

"Lorrie! Lorrie Mallard! What are you doing here?"

A car had come out of the shopping center lot across the street to draw up by her corner. Now the door swung open as Mrs. Lockner called again sharply, "Get in this minute, Lorrie. You are blue with cold. Where have you been? Where is your aunt?"

Lorrie sighed, there was no escape now. Reluctantly she got in beside Mrs. Lockner.

"Aunt Margaret had to work this morning. I just came to the library."

"By yourself? Did your aunt say you might?"

"I came on the bus. It was all right," Lorrie said defensively. "My books were due."

"But, Lorrie, you must have known I was coming to the center, you should have come with us. My, look at the time! I must swing around by Elsmere and pick up Kathy at dancing class, then get home in time to see Rob off for the game! What a big book, Lorrie. Isn't that too heavy for you?"

"I like it, and I can carry it all right." As always Mrs. Lockner's voice did something to Lorrie. She asked a lot of questions, and for anyone else Lorrie would have answered them without resentment, or at least with not as much as Mrs. Lockner always aroused in her.

"I do hope Kathy will be ready." Mrs. Lockner drove a couple of blocks before she turned right. "They are practicing for their recital and sometimes the class runs overtime. Kathy has a solo, she is going to be a gypsy."

"She told me," Lorrie said. "And she showed me her costume."

Lorrie did not envy Kathy in the least her Saturday mornings at dancing school, but that costume was another matter. Dressing up was fun, one of the things her friend Anne and she had shared in the old days when Grandmother had allowed them to dip into one of the attic trunks.

"There. Oh, thank goodness, Kathy's waiting! Just open the door for her, dear. We have

27

to travel if we are going to get Rob off on time."

So Lorrie was swept up and carried away by the Lockners. She shared their lunch, her protests being brushed aside. But she refused to share Kathy's plans for the afternoon, to go to the double monster feature at the movies.

At Lorrie's plea of having homework to do, Mrs. Lockner shook her head. But, since she could not push Lorrie out of the door with Kathy, she accepted it. Once Lorrie was back in Aunt Margaret's apartment, she got out her school books and started in on her homework. The mathematics she did first, because she hated it so. Always get the bad out of the way, then you could enjoy the good.

The good today was to write a theme about fall for English. And Lorrie knew just what she was going to write this time, about leaves and bonfires. Leaves—that made her think about Octagon House. My, the big wind today must be whirling them around. Would Hallie ever try to rake them up? Maybe Lorrie could offer to help.

She was making a neater copy of her first draft when she heard Aunt Margaret's key in the door. She was so pleased with her labors that she went eagerly to meet her, the scribbled-over first sheets in her hand.

"Aunt Margaret, I—"

But Aunt Margaret was frowning. She balanced a big grocery bag against her side and walked past Lorrie into the kitchen.

"Shut the door, Lorrie, and come here. I want to talk to you."

Lorrie obeyed. When she came to the kitchen, Aunt Margaret had taken off her coat and was sitting on one of the dinette benches. She looked tired and the frown made two sharp lines between her eyes.

"Lorrie, Mrs. Lockner spoke to me just now. She told me that you went to the library alone on the bus and that she found you standing on a street corner near the shopping center."

"I was at the bus stop there," Lorrie protested.

"I don't know what to do with you, Lorrie." Aunt Margaret had taken off her gloves, was smoothing them back and forth between her fingers. "I want to spend more time with you, but I can't. Mrs. Lockner has been very kind. She is perfectly willing for you to stay over there with Kathy when I am not at home. She would have given you a ride to the library."

"I didn't want to go with the Lockners."

"Lorrie, you can't have your way about such things. It is not safe for girls your age to go about alone. All sorts of accidents can happen. And you are alone too much. Mrs. Lockner said that Kathy wanted you to go to the show with her this afternoon and you would not."

"It was an old monster picture and I don't like them. And I had my homework to do." Lorrie crumpled her papers in her hand.

"I am not going to argue with you, Lorrie.

But neither am I going to allow you to continue in this way. From now on, when I am not at home, you are to go to Mrs. Lockner's—until I can make other arrangements."

Aunt Margaret stood up and picked up her coat. She went to the hallway and Lorrie trailed her, appalled at this idea of a future spent always with Kathy, and Rob, and probably Jimmy Purvis, too, he being one of Rob's close friends.

As she passed the coffee table, Aunt Margaret paused by the library books.

"To make this clearer, Lorrie, these books are going into the closet to stay until you prove you can be trusted to do what is right." And she took them both.

Lorrie listlessly put her school books and papers together. It wasn't fair! Kathy was one kind of person and she another. If she had to be with Kathy all the time, she couldn't stand it! And—and she would never get to visit Octagon House again.

That was the beginning of the bad week, and it seemed to Lorrie that it was never going to have an end. She went to school with Kathy and had to take part in a basketball game, which she detested. Her awkwardness always brought down upon her the impatience of her teammates. She made a poor mark in math, and Mrs. Raymond said her fall leaves story was fanciful but had too many spelling mistakes. Jimmy Purvis sang his hideous song in the yard and some of the girls picked it up. And Aunt Margaret questioned her a lot about school and how many friends she had and why didn't she do this or that, even saying she was going to have a serious talk with Mrs. Raymond.

Lorrie felt as if she were tied up in a bag, with no chance to be herself. By Friday night she was so unhappy that she felt she could not stand much more.

But on Friday the worst of all happened. Because Aunt Margaret had said she must stay at the Lockners' after school, Lorrie had had to take some of her things over there. And this time she brought the small, old lap desk Grandmother Mallard had given her. She wanted to write Grandmother a very special letter, not a complaining one, because Dr. Creighton had explained to Lorrie carefully when Grandmother had had to go to England that she must not be worried in any way.

Because this had been such a bad week, Lorrie had been afraid to write for fear some complaints might seep in despite her efforts. But she wrote Grandmother regularly and must not wait any longer. She had a first draft on notebook paper and must make another on the special paper Grandmother had given her with her name at the top of each sheet.

Lorrie laid her paper out on the card table Mrs. Lockner allowed her to set up. Then the phone rang and Mrs. Lockner called her to answer because it was Aunt Margaret saying she would be detained until late and to stay where she was.

There was no use in protesting, but Lorrie was unhappy as she came back. Then her eyes went wide and all the unhappiness of the week exploded inside her.

"Give me that!" She grabbed at what Kathy had taken from the desk.

"Let me look first." Kathy, laughing, jumped away, swinging her hand out of Lorrie's reach. "What a funny old doll. You still play with dolls, Lorrie? Only little kids do that."

In her grasp the old doll dangled too loosely. The delicate china head struck hard against the wall and smashed into pieces.

"Miranda!" Lorrie sprang at Kathy, standing disconcerted now over the broken bits of china. She slapped her as hard as she could. "Give me—!"

"All right, take it!" Kathy threw the headless body at Lorrie and it sprawled half in, half out, of the writing desk.

Lorrie scooped up desk and all and ran out of the Lockner apartment. She was fumbling with her own key when Mrs. Lockner caught up with her.

"Lorrie, what is the matter? Tell me at once!"

Lorrie struggled against the hand on her shoulder. "Let me alone! Can't you *ever* let me alone!" She was crying now in spite of her efforts not to.

"Why did you slap Kathy? Lorrie, tell me, what is the matter?"

"Let me alone!" The key was in the lock now. With a sharp jerk Lorrie freed herself from Mrs. Lockner's hold and got around the door. The writing desk and the paper fell all over the floor, but those did not matter now. What did, she still held in her arm tight against her chest.

Lorrie turned and slammed the door right in Mrs. Lockner's face, locking it quickly. She heard them calling, knocking on the door. Let everyone yell and bang—it wouldn't do them any good! Crying so hard she could hardly see, Lorrie made the bedroom and flung herself on her bed. She felt the hard lump of Miranda under her, but she could not bear now to look at that headless body.

Miranda had been extra special. She was not just a doll, but a person, and she was very, very old. Grandmother had played with her when she was little, very carefully, because even then Miranda was special. Grandmother's own grandmother had had Miranda. She was more than a hundred years old! Now—now—Miranda wasn't anything!

Lorrie rolled over on the bed and made herself look at the remains. The small arms and hands of leather were intact, and the black boots and legs covered with red-and-white striped stockings were as always. But, above the old-fashioned dress Grandmother had made, the head and shoulders were gone, only one little jagged splinter was left. Miranda was dead and Kathy had killed her! She would never, never speak to Kathy Lockner again! Nor would she ever go back to the Lockner apartment.

Still gulping sobs, she got off the bed and went to the chest of drawers. She found the handkerchief Grandmother had given her. That was old, too, soft heavy silk, yellow now, with a big, fat initial G and some marks over it embroidered in one corner. It had belonged to Grandmother's father.

Tenderly she wrapped Miranda in it. Miranda was dead and Lorrie could not bear to look at her again. They might even say to throw her out in the trash, just an old broken doll. But Miranda was not going into any trash can, she was going to be buried where there were flowers in summer.

And the place—the Octagon House! Lorrie put on her coat and cap. She opened the back service door and, with Miranda in her hand, crept down the back steps. It was getting dark out, but she did not have far to go. In her other hand was the big spoon she had picked up in the kitchen. She could dig a grave with that. She only hoped the ground was not frozen too hard.

Lorrie ran across the parking lot and out the other end, and came to the gate that she had climbed on her first visit. There were no lights at all in the house that she could see, and the bushes and trees made it seem very dark. But Lorrie was too unhappy to be afraid.

Hallie had done something to the upper bar of the gate to open it. But then Hallie had been on the other side. Lorrie had best climb again. She had laid her hand on the gate to do just that when it gave and swung a little, easier than when Hallie had opened it for her. Then she stood on the shadow-patched brick walk.

The flower beds in the back—they ought to be easier to dig in. Heedless of the shadows, Lorrie hurried to the place by the pool. There she squatted to dig with her spoon.

There was no wind tonight, so she heard the tapping sharp and clear. Lorrie turned her head to look at the house. There were the windows with the curtains. And now there was a light there, not bright, but enough to show the lady who was leaning forward with her face quite close to the glass. And it was not Hallie.

For a long moment Lorrie was startled, too startled to run as she might have done. Then she saw that the lady was not frowning or looking in the least cross as she might have been at someone digging in her garden. Instead she smiled, and now she beckoned to Lorrie, and pointed in the direction of the back door.

Lorrie hesitated and then got to her feet, still pressing Miranda close to her. Then the lady tapped again and once more pointed. Lorrie obeyed, walking along the brick path.

The door swung open before she had quite reached the steps, and Hallie greeted her. "Mis' Lorrie, come in, come! Mis' Ashmeade, she wants to see you."

Lorrie came into a hall that had darkish corners in spite of a lamp set up on a wall bracket. It was triangular in shape with a door in each wall. One opened into a kitchen, and Lorrie could see part of a stove. The other, to her right, opened into the room off the curtained windows. Hallie pointed to that.

"Go right in."

Lorrie suddenly felt very shy. The lady in the window had smiled and seemed friendly, but she had not invited her in.

It was the strangest room Lorrie had ever seen. The light there, and there was light in plenty, all came from lamps and candles that flickered now and then. There were red-velvet drapes at the windows over white-lace curtains, and a red carpet underfoot. A big table, which had two candelabra, was in the center of the room, and it had a great many things laid out on it. There was a fireplace to her left with a fire glowing in it, and before it on the hearthrug lay Sabina.

Between the table and the windows was a chair with carved arms and a high back. In it sat the lady. She wore a dress with a tight waist and a full long skirt like Hallie's. But this was an odd shade of green. And her long apron was not white and ruffled as Hallie's but made of black taffeta with a border of brilliant flowers and birds worked in many colored silks. Her hair was very white but thick, and was braided and then pinned about her head with a fluff of black lace and dark red ribbon fastened on for a cap.

She had a tall frame at her elbow as if she had just turned away from her work. And on that was stretched canvas with a picture half embroidered. But now her hands rested on the arms of her chair, and on their fingers were many rings, most of them set with the red stones Lorrie knew for garnets such as Grandmother had, but seldom wore.

A necklace of the same stones lay on the front of her dress, and earrings glinted in her ears. She did not look at all like any lady Lorrie had ever seen, but in this room she belonged.

"Come here, Lorrie. Let me see Miranda." She held out her hand and her rings winked in the firelight.

Lorrie did not find it odd that Miss Ashemeade should know just what she carried in her bundle of handkerchief.

Miss Ashemeade put one hand over the other, the package that was Miranda between her palms. For a long moment she sat so, then she spoke:

"There is breaking in plenty in this world, Lorrie. But there is also mending, if one has will and patience. Never be hasty, for haste may sometimes make a large trouble from a small one. Now, what do you think of that?"

She pointed to something that lay across one end of the table. Lorrie moved a little to see a length of lace, so delicate and beautiful that, though she would like to touch it, she did not quite dare. It was a cobweb, as if some spider had chosen to spin a design instead of her usual back-and-forth lines. But there was a breaking of threads, a tear to spoil it.

"Haste makes waste." Miss Ashemeade shook her head. "Now much time and patience must be used to mend it."

"But Miranda can't be," Lorrie said. "Her head was all smashed, into little bits."

"We shall see." Still she did not unwrap Miranda to look. "Now, Lorrie, tell me, what do you see here? Take your time and look well. But"—now Miss Ashemeade smiled—"remember something that was a command of my youth— look with your eyes and not your fingers."

Lorrie nodded. "Don't touch," she translated. She might have resented such a warning, she was no baby. But somehow it was right and proper here. Now she began to look about her, moving around the room.

It was exciting, for there was a great deal to see. On the walls hung framed pictures, many of them too dim to make out clearly, though Lorrie saw some were strips of cloth and the

painting had been done with needle and thread
rather than paint and brush. Across the back of
a sofa was a square of fine crossstitch, a bouquet
of flowers. And the seats and backs of every chair
were worked in similar patterns.

Over the fireplace was a tapestry that drew
and held Lorrie's full attention. A knight and his
squire rode toward a wood, while in the foreground stood a girl wearing a dress of the same
shade of green as Miss Ashemeade had chosen.
Her feet were bare, her dark hair flowed freely
about her shoulders from under a garland of
pale flowers.

"That is the Tapestry Princess."

Lorrie looked around. "Is it a story?" she
asked.

"It is a story, Lorrie. And the moral of it is,
or was, make the best of what you have, do with
it what you can, but do not throw away your
dreams. Once that princess was a daughter of a
king. She was given everything her heart wished.
Then her father fell upon evil days, and she was
captured by his enemy and put in a tower. All
she had left her was one of her christening gifts,
a golden needle her godmother had given her.

"She learned to sew in order to mend her own
old clothing. And so beautiful was her work that
the usurper, who had taken her father's throne,
had her make clothing for his daughters, the
new princesses. She grew older and older and no
one cared.

"Then she began at night to make the tapestry. First she fashioned the knight and squire. And then worked all the background, except for one space in the foreground. One of the usurper's daughters, coming to try on a dress, saw the tapestry and ordered the princess to make haste to finish it, that she might have it to hang on the wall at her wedding feast.

"So the princess worked the whole night through to complete it. And the maiden she put into the blank space was she as she had been when she was a young and beautiful girl. When the last stitch was set she vanished from the tower, nor was she ever found again."

"Did she go into the tapestry?" Lorrie asked.

"So it is said. But it is true she found some way of freedom and only her picture remained to remind the world of her story. Now, Lorrie, you have a story, too. And what is it?"

Without knowing just why, Lorrie spilled out all that had happened during the bad week, and some of the other things that had been bothering her for what seemed now to be a long, long time.

"And you say that you hate Kathy, you really do, my dear? Because she broke Miranda?"

Lorrie looked at the silken bundle in Miss Ashemeade's lap.

"No, I guess I don't really hate her. And I—I guess I'm sorry I slapped her. She didn't mean to break Miranda."

"Hate is a big and hard word, Lorrie. Don't use it unless you are sure. You have been unhappy and so have seen only unhappy things around you. You have been setting your stitches crooked, and now they must be picked out again. Such picking must always be done or the design will be spoiled."

"I wish"—Lorrie looked about her longingly —"I wish I could stay here."

"You do not want to go back to Aunt Margaret?" All at once there was a sharp note in Miss Ashemeade's voice.

"Oh, no, I don't mean that. I guess I mean I wish I could just come here sometimes."

Miss Ashemeade beckoned to her. "Come here, child."

Lorrie edged around the table, came directly before Miss Ashemeade, on one side of her the frame holding the unfinished work, and on the other a table whose top was set up as a lid to show many small compartments, all filled with spools and reels of brightly colored silk and wool thread.

Her chin was cupped in Miss Ashemeade's hand as the old lady leaned forward to look into her eyes. It seemed to Lorrie that all her thoughts were being read, and suddenly she was ashamed of some of them. She wanted to turn away her eyes, but she could not.

Then Miss Ashemeade nodded. "Perhaps

something may be arranged. Now, Lorrie, I shall write a note for you to take to your aunt, that she will know where you have been. Miranda you shall leave with me, which is better than burying her in my herb garden, as you thought to do."

Ride a White Horse

LORRIE shuffled her feet unhappily as she came up the hall of the apartment. But she knew what she had to do and pushed the button beside the Lockner door, feeling that if she did not do it at once she might turn and run. Then she was looking at Kathy and she said in a fast rush of words:

"I'm sorry I slapped you."

"Mom, it's Lorrie! Hey, your aunt's here. They've been looking all over for you." Kathy caught at her arm. "Listen, Mom gave me heck for breaking your doll. I didn't mean to, really."

Lorrie nodded. Aunt Margaret now stood behind Kathy. She looked at Lorrie with no welcoming smile. Rather she put her hand out in turn and set it firmly on Lorrie's shoulders.

"Come, Lorrie. I believe you have something to say to Mrs. Lockner also, haven't you?"

Again Lorrie nodded. There was a tight knot of misery in her throat that made her voice hoarse as she said to Mrs. Lockner:

"I'm sorry. I shouldn't have slapped Kathy, or run away."

"No, you should not. But then Kathy should not have taken your doll either, Lorrie. Your aunt has explained that it meant a lot to you. Where is it? Perhaps it can be mended."

"No." Lorrie found it very hard to look at Mrs. Lockner. "I don't have her any more."

"I believe Lorrie has caused enough trouble today, Mrs. Lockner. We'll go home now."

Aunt Margaret's hand propelled Lorrie to their own apartment. Once inside, her aunt moved away from her, leaving Lorrie standing alone. Aunt Margaret sat down with a sigh. For a moment she rested her head on her hand, her eyes closed, and she looked very tired indeed. Lorrie fumbled with the zipper on her windbreaker, let it slip off her arms and shoulders. It tumbled to the floor and the small envelope Miss Ashemeade had given her fell from the pocket. Lorrie picked it up and stood turning it in her hands.

"I don't know what to do with you, Lorrie. This running away, and slapping Kathy Lockner. She was only interested in your doll. If you did not want to show her Miranda, why did you take the doll over there?"

"Miranda was in my desk. I took that over to write a letter to Grandmother."

If Aunt Margaret heard her, she did not seem to care. She sighed again and got up as if it were an effort to move.

"I am too tired to talk to you now, Lorrie. Go to your room and think about this afternoon, think about it carefully."

Aunt Margaret started for the kitchen.

"But I haven't set the table."

"I believe I can manage very well without your help. I want you to spend some time thinking, Lorrie. Now!"

Slowly Lorrie went to the bedroom. She had laid the letter on the coffee table. That did not matter now. Aunt Margaret was angry or, what was worse, hurt. Lorrie sat down on the bench before the dressing table and stared at her reflection in the mirror, and then she covered her face with her hands.

Think about this afternoon, Aunt Margaret said. It was hard now for her to understand what *had* happened, even harder to puzzle out why. She had not wanted to go to the Lockners', and then Kathy with Miranda . . . and the shattering crash of Miranda's head against the wall . . . her hand against Kathy's cheek. Then planning to bury Miranda . . . going to Octagon House, meeting with Miss Ashemeade—What had Miss Ashemeade said?

"Haste makes waste—"

46

Lorrie took a tissue from the box in the top drawer to wipe her eyes and blow her nose. She was sorry about Kathy and about causing Mrs. Lockner and Aunt Margaret trouble. But she was not sorry about meeting Miss Ashemeade —she was glad for that.

"Lorrie," Aunt Margaret called.

"Coming." Lorrie gave a last wipe to her reddened eyes.

Aunt Margaret was already seated at the table as Lorrie slid in across from her. Friday night was usually a night when they had special food and a happy time, but not tonight. Lorrie sighed.

"Aunt Margaret—" That knot in her throat was back, so big a lump that she could not swallow anything, even a sip of hot chocolate. "I'm sorry."

"Yes, I believe you are—now—Lorrie. But being sorry now, will that last so something such as this does not happen again? You know I cannot be with you as I would like. And you cannot stay alone. Mrs. Lockner has been more than kind, considering your rudeness in return."

Lorrie choked, staring down at the plate of food she could not eat.

"Lorrie, I know that this way of living is very different from what you had with Grandmother Mallard. But to sulk because of that—I do not like it."

Lorrie felt for the tissue in her pocket.

"You cannot expect to have friends if you are

not friendly in turn. When Kathy asks you to go places with her you always say no. You have not joined any of the school clubs. Mrs. Raymond tells me that at recess you sit and read a book, unless the playground teacher asks you, or rather orders you, to join in a game. I know that this was all strange to you when you came. But surely it is not so now and you should be making friends."

Aunt Margaret pushed aside her own plate as if she could not swallow any better than Lorrie. She drank her coffee slowly, the frown lines between her eyes very sharp.

"What did you do with Miranda?" she asked abruptly.

"I took her to the Octagon House," Lorrie answered, hardly above a whisper.

"The—the Octagon House?" Aunt Margaret sounded really surprised. "But why in the world?"

"I wanted to bury Miranda, not just throw her out in the trash. There's a garden there."

"How do you know that?"

Then Lorrie told about the kitten and the meeting with Hallie, and of today when she had seen Miss Ashemeade in her wonderful room. As she poured out her story, some of her misery eased and she could look at Aunt Margaret again.

"And she sent you a note—" Lorrie dashed into the other room, came back with the envelope, which she laid before Aunt Margaret.

Her aunt opened it. Lorrie caught a glimpse

of the writing, very different from any she had ever seen, looped and curved as much as the decorations of the rusty iron gate.

Aunt Margaret read it twice and her frown became a puzzled look. She studied the signature again before she turned to Lorrie.

"Miss Ashemeade—would like you to spend the day with her tomorrow."

Could she go? Lorrie did not quite dare ask. Not to go—that might be what Aunt Margaret would consider a suitable punishment for this bad week. Oh, if she could go, she would be willing to do whatever they wanted her to— go to the monster show with Kathy, play basketball, all the things she shrank from but which they seemed to think she should want to do. But she could not ask or promise, somehow she could not. She did not know the brightness of her eyes, the strained look on her face asked for her.

"Very well." Aunt Margaret folded the note to slip back into the envelope. "You may go." Then, as if that decision had lifted a big black shadow from the kitchen, she began to eat. Lorrie swallowed. The knot was gone from her throat too. Suddenly she was hungry and everything looked good.

She did all her homework that evening, being twice as careful with the math problems, while Aunt Margaret worked with her own papers and sketches on the other side of the table. Lorrie picked up one drawing that had somehow been mixed in with her scribble sheets. She looked at a chair that was familiar and then realized she had seen its like in Miss Ashemeade's room. Only this was painted with a golden covering, and she thought the needlework of flowers much prettier.

"Why don't they have flowers here?" She held out the sketch. "Miss Ashemeade does—pink, yellow, and green—a pale green—" For a moment Lorrie closed her eyes to picture the better her memory of the chair.

"You saw a chair such as this at Miss Ashemeade's?"

Lorrie opened her eyes. Her aunt was staring at her in surprise.

"Yes. She has two. They are by the fireplace. But hers have embroidered backs and seats."

"What colors did you say?"

"Well, the background is not quite light yellow, more cream. And the flowers are not bright, but you can see them. There are pink roses, and some small yellow bell things, and they're in a bunch tied with ribbon—the ribbon is pink, too. Then they have a circle of leaves, a kind of vine, around them, and it is a pale green."

Her aunt nodded. "Probably petit point. But it is an excellent idea—we want to use this chair as a background for a sketch of formal gowns. Lorrie, when you are there tomorrow look carefully at those colors, and the design. Do you know, from what you have told me, you are a very fortunate girl. Miss Ashemeade's house must be a treasury of fine old things."

"It's beautiful, simply beautiful!" Lorrie cried. "And the candles—the fire— It's just wonderful!"

Aunt Margaret smiled as she put her papers back in her briefcase. "I can imagine that it is. Now, you might try making tomorrow come the sooner by getting to bed."

Lorrie thought that it might be as hard to get to sleep as it was on Christmas Eve. But it did not turn out that way, for she was so quickly asleep that afterward she could not remember climbing into bed. And morning did arrive swiftly after all.

She managed her share of the morning work eagerly and then decided that a visit of such import demanded her go-to-tea dress. That seemed tight now and Aunt Margaret, looking her over before Lorrie put on her best coat, agreed that she must have grown since Grandmother had had it made.

Then she was free, speeding along Ash Street at anything but a decorous pace, toward Octagon House. Again the gate gave to her push and she walked more soberly around to the door, which Hallie opened promptly at her knock.

"She's havin' her mornin' chocolate, you go right in. There's a cup waitin' for you, too, Mis' Lorrie."

Then she was back in the red-velvet room.

The drapes were pulled back to let in the fall sunshine. There was still a fire going, but no need for candles this morning.

Miss Ashmeade's chair had been moved closer to the window, so the daylight fell across her frame and the contents of the table which held the silks and wools. But before her was another small table and on it sat a tall, straight-sided pot with violets scattered over its white sides and gold edging on its handle. Two cups matching the pot sat on a small tray, and there was a plate with a fringed napkin covering it.

"Good morning, Lorrie."

Lorrie had hesitated just within the door. Now she curtsied.

"Good morning, Miss Ashemeade." She must watch her manners. This was a room which welcomed only the most ladylike behavior.

"Give Hallie your coat and hat, my dear. Do you like chocolate?"

Lorrie wriggled out of her outdoor things. "Yes, please."

At Miss Ashemeade's gesture she sat down on a high stool across from her hostess. Miss Ashemeade poured from the tall pot, and took the napkin from the plate to display some small biscuits. Lorrie sipped her chocolate from a cup so light and delicate that she feared an incautious touch might break it. Then she nibbled at a biscuit that was crisp and not sweet, but which had

a flavor all its own, one she had never tasted
before.

"Do ycu know how to sew, Lorrie?" asked
Miss Ashemeade as she emptied her own cup.

"A little. Grandmother was teaching me to
make Miranda a dress."

"There was a lady in England," Miss Ashemeade replied, "who once said that it was as
disgraceful for a lady not to know how to use a
needle as it was for a gentleman to be ignorant
of how to handle his sword." She wiped her
fingers on a small napkin. Lorrie did not know
just what was expected of her, but she said after
a moment's pause:

"Gentlemen do not have swords any more."

"No. Nor do many ladies use needles either.
But to forget or set aside any art is an unhappy
thing."

Miss Ashemeade glanced around at the pictures, the rolls of material on the long table, to
the tapestry over the fireplace. Then she picked
up a silver bell, which gave a tinkle and brought
Hallie in to take the tray.

For the first time Lorrie saw the top of the
table on which the chocolate set had rested.
Against a black background was a scene that
held her attention. There was a gold castle on
a mountain, its windows all pearl, while above it
a moon of the same pearl peered out of golden
clouds. Miss Ashemeade saw her interest and
traced the scene with a finger tip.

"Papier-mâché, my dear. Once it was very popular. Now, Lorrie, suppose you put this little table over there, since we no longer need it."

The table was very light, Lorrie discovered, and she could easily move it. When she came back, Miss Ashemeade was bending over the table with all the small compartments under its top lid. She had pulled around before her the frame with the half-finished work, and now Lorrie could see that that was a picture, too, within a flower border.

"Do you think you can help me a little?" Miss Ashemeade asked.

"Oh, yes!" Lorrie was eager.

You may thread my needles, if you will." Miss Ashemeade smiled. "I can no longer see as well as I once did, and needle threading is a trial at times. Now, here are the needles in this case. And I will use threads this long, from this, and this, and this." She pointed to the colored wools wound smoothly on reels of carved ivory.

Lorrie set to work. The needles were fine, but they had larger eyes than any she had seen before, so threading was not hard. There were quite a few needles standing up in the funny little ivory case made like a cat—you unscrewed its head to see them. But that was not the only needle box in the table compartments. Miss Ashemeade took out the other one and opened it. Inside there was room for many needles to be stuck through a piece of green velvet, but only two were there. They were different from the ones Lorrie threaded, for they gleamed of gold in the sunlight instead of silver.

"There, Lorrie"—Miss Ashemeade's voice was serious—"are very special needles and not to be often used."

"They look like gold," Lorrie ventured.

"They are," answered Miss Ashemeade. "And they are very important."

"Like the magic needles the princess had?"

"Just so. You will not use them, Lorrie. Understand?"

"Yes, Miss Ashemeade."

As Miss Ashemeade closed that case and put it back, Lorrie noted that it was of a dark wood that looked very, very old, and it was patterned on the top with tarnished metal.

"Thank you, Lorrie. Now you may stick those all along the frame where they may be easily reached. You have been sitting still, which I know is hard for one of your years. So, now you are free to explore."

"Explore?" echoed Lorrie.

"Explore the house. You are free, Lorrie, to enter any room where the door will open for you."

What a queer thing to say, Lorrie thought. As if a door could choose of itself whether or not to open for her. But to explore the house, yes, that was exciting.

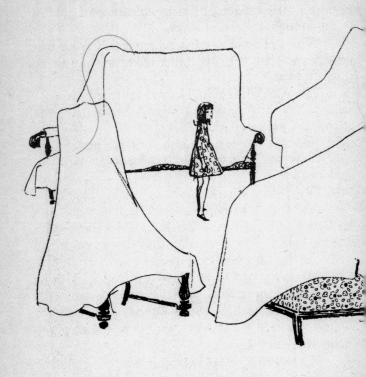

"Thank you."

Miss Ashemeade smiled again. "Thank me when you return, Lorrie, if you still wish to."

That, too, was puzzling. But Lorrie did not try to figure it out. She decided to leave by the

door opposite the one where she had entered.
Miss Ashemeade was bending over the frame,
already beginning to stitch the canvas.

Lorri went into the next room. This was
dusky, behind the closed shutters. Unlike Miss

Ashemeade's warm and welcoming chamber, this was chill and dark. No fire burned in the fireplace. All the furniture was covered by sheets.

Lorrie glanced around. The room had let her enter, but there was very little to see that attracted her. Next was a hallway, and then another room, which must balance the red room. It was a bedroom and it was alive and open, only it was all green—as green as Miss Ashemeade's dress. The bed was very large and had carved posts and a frame at the top of them, from which hung pale green curtains patterned with vines in darker green, the same shade as the carpet under Lorrie's feet. There were chairs and a small sofa, all covered in light green patterned with the darker leaves. Almost, Lorrie thought, one could believe this a wood with things growing.

She stood by the foot of the bed, looking about her. Miss Ashemeade had said to enter any room that would let her. But Lorrie did not feel comfortable here.

"Merrow—"

Lorrie, startled, looked to her left. There were two other doors leading out of the room, and peering about the edge of the nearer was Sabina. She opened her small mouth again to utter a cry that sounded much too large for such a small kitten, almost, Lorrie decided, as if she were impatiently telling her to hurry.

As Lorrie went toward her, Sabina ducked around the door and disappeared. Then Lorrie entered.

She was in a very queerly shaped small room. The outer wall, which had a single window, met the longer wall to her right at a very sharp and narrow angle. But on the other side, to her left, it was square as an ordinary room. There were no curtains or drapes, so the light came through easily to show what stood there.

60

Lorrie gasped. The center of the misshapen room was occupied by an eight-sided dias or platform of polished wood. Set in the sides of that were drawers, each marked by a gleaming brass keyhole and handles. And using that base for a foundation was a house of red brick with a wooden trim, an exact copy of the very home in which it stood. If it were a doll house it was larger and more perfect than any Lorrie had seen before. Taller than Lorrie herself, it almost filled the room.

Facing what was meant to be the front door of the house was a rocking horse such as Lorrie had seen pictured in the old volumes of the *St. Nicholas* magazines. It was big, nearly as large as a pony she had ridden at the park last summer, and it was white, with a silky mane. On its back was a red saddle. Only, Lorrie saw as she went closer, it was an oddly shaped saddle, not like any she had seen before.

She put out her hand cautiously. Why, the horse felt as if he were covered with real hide! Bolder, Lorrie stroked his mane, and under her touch he rocked back and forth with a faint creak-creak.

"Merrow!" Sabina was standing on her hind legs, as if she were trying to peep into one of the windows. But it was too high above her head. Lorrie went on her knees to look too.

It was as if she were viewing a real house through the wrong end of field glasses, making all

61

smaller instead of larger. There was furniture and pictures, and carpets on the floor. She could even see a little tea table with a service set out upon it, just waiting for someone to pour. In fact, as Lorrie moved around the house, she had the oddest feeling that it was inhabited, and, if she hurried a little faster, she would catch sight of some person who had just this moment left the room into which she was now looking.

Miss Ashemeade's red-velvet room was different, for in the little house it was a dining room, the long table set with a white cloth and dishes ready for a meal. She crawled around to the kitchen side and then on to look into the green bedroom. Upstairs there were other bedrooms —three big square ones. And then there were three triangular rooms that had big cupboards in them, and another, oddly shaped room with a stair opening into it.

All of it was furnished and ready—so ready. The oven in the kitchen stove was half ajar and she could see the end of a loaf of bread.

Doll houses opened, so this must. How else could all the furniture have been put in? But when Lorrie tried to find any hinge or latch on the outside she could not. Baffled, she sat back on her heels. Then she tugged at the pulls on the base drawers. But not one gave to her urging. They had keyholes, perhaps they were locked.

Once more she circled the house. It was just a little taller than she was, counting the base.

But the attic rooms were so dark she could not
see in through their slits of windows. If there
were any rooms behind those they remained a
mystery. Maybe the house was to be respected as
Miss Ashemeade had warned her, something to
look at with the eyes but not with the fingers.
And there was plenty to look at, tiny marvels in
each room every time she peered anew.

Lorrie stepped back. She could not rid herself
of the belief that this was no ordinary doll house
to be played with. It was so much like the house
in which it stood that somehow it was alive,
really more alive than those parts of Octagon
House she had found sheeted and covered. And

there remained her feeling that all of the smaller house, not just part of it, was in use—by someone.

Used by what—whom? She hurried around the corner to look into another window, then raced to the next room. If she could just move fast enough to catch a glimpse of the tiny person who only that moment had gone out! Then she stood still and looked at Sabina, who had settled down in the full light of the window, to wash a back paw with deliberation and much attention to the space between two well-spread toes.

"It's—it's just a doll house, isn't it, Sabina? No one *does* live there. No one could."

Sabina did not even flick an ear in her direction. Lorrie took another step back and her shoulder struck against the rocking horse. He swayed, and under the rocker the floor creaked. Lorrie drew her hand down his mane. Just—almost as good as a pony.

She eyed the queer saddle. Why was it made that way? But—it would be fun to take a ride. Rocking horses were for little kids, but this was such a big one.

Lorrie climbed on and tried to sit astride the saddle. But you could not do that comfortably, it had bumps in the wrong places. Somehow, she did not know how, she found herself sitting the horse in another way, her knee hooked over a big horn, both of her feet on the same side of the horse. And he began to rock, faster—

There was a wind blowing and leaves whirled up—leaves? Lorrie blinked. This was not the room, it was a road with trees on either side and the wind in their branches. She was not on a rocking horse at all, but on a real one. And she wore a long skirt flapping in the wind. For a moment she was stiff with fright, and then that fright vanished. Dimly she had a strange feeling she had done this before, that this was just as it should be.

The white horse moved easily at a steady trot, and Lorrie rode him as if this was the most natural thing in the world. Not too far ahead was a brick house. The Octagon House! Lorrie's heart beat faster. Something, someone was waiting there for her and it was most important.

Then the horse flung up his head and shook it. He stopped beside a big block of stone by an iron gate. Lorrie slipped out of the saddle to the stone and then to the ground. She had to gather the long folds of her skirt up over her arm or she would have tripped on them. But she opened the gate and walked up to the front door.

There was a brass knocker there and Lorrie lifted it, letting it fall again with a loud bang. Only—there was no answer. No one came, and when she tried the door it was locked. Her happy excitement was gone, suddenly she shivered and was afraid.

The wind blew dust at her and she closed her eyes. When she opened them there was no big door. She stood in front of the doll house. Her long skirt had vanished, everything was as it had been. Lorrie blinked rapidly. It was a dream, that was what it had been. But—she looked about the room—she did not want to stay in here any more.

Nor did she want to explore any further. Swiftly she retraced her way back to the red room. There was only one threaded needle still unused at the side of the frame. Miss Ashemeade looked up as Lorrie hurried to the light of the window. It seemed to Lorrie as if in that glance Miss Ashemeade had learned all that had happened. She did not want to talk of the small house, or of the horse, not even to Miss Ashemeade.

"Well, my dear, see, I have almost finished my morning's stint. Do you know what a stint is?"

"No." Lorrie sat down on the stool.

"When I was young every little girl had a piece of needlework on which she did an allotted portion of work each day. That was her stint. It was an excellent way in which to learn both discipline and sewing."

She took up the last of the needles Lorrie had threaded. "Now, just this last small bit—"

"Oh!" Lorrie cried out in admiration.

In the picture there was now a small fawn standing beside the tree that had marked the edge of the filled space when she had come that morning. It was so real! Lorrie felt that if she put out a finger she would touch sun-warmed hide.

"You like it?"

"It is so real."

"Would you like to learn to do this?"

"Could I? Could I really make something—a picture?"

Again Miss Ashemeade gave her one of those long, piercing looks. "Not without a great deal of patience and hard work, Lorrie. And no haste, you must understand, no haste."

"Could I try?" Lorrie was only a little daunted.

"We can always try—anything," Miss Ashemeade answered. "Yes, you may try, Lorrie. You may begin this afternoon if you wish. But in the beginning you do not do this kind of work. Beginning is sometimes very dull and takes learning and practice."

"I would like to try, please," Lorrie said.

"Then you shall, and we will see if you have any gift for it. Now, dear, will you tell Hallie we are ready for lunch?"

Phineas and Phebe

AFTER that Saturday Lorrie found she was living two lives. But it was not confusing. In one she was Lorrie Mallard who went to school, who did her homework, who walked home with Kathy now and then, who had household tasks to do. But to be that Lorrie was not too hard because there was escape into Octagon House. She did not go too often, of course, though she tried to take the alley route by it each morning and evening, hurrying before and after that one stretch of walk so she could go more slowly there. And twice Hallie had been at the chained back gate with a note for Aunt Margaret, inviting Lorrie to more afternoons in Miss Ashemeade's big room.

Miss Ashemeade had been very right in her warning that to learn to sew was a task. The needles and silks and wools never seemed to prick *her* fingers or tangle when she used them. Sometimes she worked on the canvas in the frame, or again she mended lace or one of the pieces that lay waiting on the table. But she was never too busy to look over Lorrie's strip of linen on which were shaping rows of different kinds of stitches. That "sampler" would serve Lorrie later, Miss Ashemeade said, as a pattern for all the stitches one must know.

Sometimes as they worked together Miss Ashemeade told stories. And sometimes Lorrie talked about Grandmother Mallard and Miss Logan's, and once even about Mother and Father. And sometimes about school.

"I'm to be a Puritan," she announced on her third visit. "It's for the Thanksgiving play. I don't have anything to say. I just bring in a big dish of pretend corn for the table. We're supposed to be giving a feast with the Indians as guests."

Miss Ashemeade was working on the lace, using the finest of thread and needles. Even Lorrie's bright eyes had had trouble in finding the holes in those.

"Indians and Puritans. So you are beginning to learn your American history now, Lorrie? Perhaps with less trouble?"

"Some. I still get mixed up once in a while though. And then that Jimmy Purvis always laughs."

"Jimmy Purvis." Miss Ashemeade took another

almost invisible stitch. "Ah, yes, he is the boy who chased Sabina."

"He's mean, just plain mean and hateful!" Lorrie burst out. Since she walked now and then with Kathy, Jimmy and his gang were not quite so much on her heels, but she still was a little afraid of him. "I don't like boys anyway, they're always doing mean things."

"How many boys do you know, Lorrie?"

"Well, there's Rob Lockner, he's always tagging along with Jimmy, doing what Jimmy tells him to. Then there's Stan Wormiski. He's another. There're all the boys at school. But I don't bother with them—they're all mean."

"All mean," repeated Miss Ashemeade thoughtfully. "That is quite a severe judgment, isn't it, Lorrie? But perhaps you have reason to make it. Now—" She looked around. "Sabina seems to have vanished. I wonder if you would find her for me, Lorrie?"

Since Sabina came and went at will and apparently Miss Ashemeade did not care, Lorrie wondered a little at such an errand. But she obediently put aside her sampler and went to hunt the kitten.

Through the room with the shrouded furniture she called, "Sabina, Sabina!" with no mew of answer. Then the half-ajar door brought her on to the green bedroom and finally to the strangely shaped room of the doll house and the rocking horse.

Sabina was there, all right. She was standing on three legs, while with her right forepaw she patted at one of the drawers in the base. From the keyhole there something dangled, swinging back and forth. Lorrie got down to look. And Sabina jumped to one side, as if Lorrie's coming had caught her in some mischief that she must now pretend she knew nothing about.

What swung from the keyhole was a chain, a gold chain, and it was fastened to a key set in the drawer lock. On impulse Lorrie turned the key, and the drawer pulled out easily.

Two dolls lay within upon their backs, staring up at her. One was about five inches high, the other four, and their heads were modeled with very lifelike expressions. But they were not made of china, Lorrie noticed, though they were quaint enough to seem as if they were as old, if not older than, Miranda.

The taller doll was a boy with black hair. And his clothes were odd. He wore long trousers of gray material and a short jacket fastened with a single button under his chin. The little girl had her brown hair parted in the middle and pulled back of her ears where her braids were turned up and under, pinned in a coil. She had a dress that was wide across the shoulders and veed in a point from the yoke to the high waist, and there were small frills of lace showing at neck and wrist. The skirt was full but not floor length, and under it showed pantalets much ruffled.

With great care Lorrie picked up the boy doll. The clothing was so carefully made that, having become so conscious of stitchery, she marveled at the patience taken in its making. She was going to lay him back in the drawer when she heard a faint squeak and looked up to see Sabina claw at the side of the house.

"No—"

But Lorrie was too late. The little claws touched some hidden spring and half the house moved, swinging back—the walls that covered the green bedroom and the kitchen. It moved easily though Sabina did not touch it again, but sat back to watch.

Now Lorrie could see the interior in detail, much clearer than she had through the windows. And for a long moment or two she simply looked. One of the portions now revealed was the very room in which she sat. But it did not in the least mirror the modern room. There was no rocking horse in miniature, no second doll house. Instead, on the now empty shelves along the wall were tiny books, and rows of minute jars and crocks. There was one chair in the corner—could it be a copy of the high-backed one Miss Ashemeade now used? And on the floor was a painted design instead of a carpet or rug. That resembled a star, Lorrie thought.

But the oddest thing revealed by the opening of the outer wall was a three-cornered space between this room and the kitchen. When the house wall was shut that must be completely closed, as there was no opening into it from either this room or the kitchen. What was it meant for, Lorrie wondered. A cupboard? But then why no door to it?

The kitchen absorbed her attention the most. It was in such detail. There were even baskets of vegetables and eggs on the table. And she could see the bread waiting in the oven. All it needed was a Hallie busy there to bring it to life.

On impulse she put the boy doll by the fireplace. He was able to stand, Lorrie discovered, if you fixed his feet properly. Then she added the girl and lifted the egg basket from the table to hang on her arms. There!

Carefully Lorrie swung the side of the house shut and crouched way down to peer through a window. Why, they looked real, as if they were going to move about their own business any minute. They belonged somehow just where she had put them.

There must be a reason——

Not understanding why, Lorrie got up and went to the horse. It was easier to get into the queer saddle now and she settled herself on the horse with more confidence. Under her weight he began to rock. . . .

No wind blew today along the gravel road, but it was fall and leaves lay about. The white horse trotted toward Octagon House and again Lorrie felt that rise of excitement. Something was going to happen, something important—

This time when she slid off onto the mounting block she did not go to the front door that had refused to admit her before. But, gathering her skirt up over her arm, she took the brick walk around the side. The trees and bushes growing along the fence were smaller and not tangled all together, but they made a screen. And it was a dark day with heavy clouds hanging overhead, cold in spite of the lack of wind.

Lorrie came to the back steps and held her long skirt higher so she could climb them. But when she raised her hand to knock on the door it swung and she opened it. No Hallie stood there to bid her welcome.

It was the same triangle with the two doors, one to Miss Ashemeade's room, one to the kitchen. The one to the red room was tightly closed, and when Lorrie tried to raise the old latch, it did not move. She remembered what Miss Ashemeade had said:

"You may go through any door that will let you."

But Miss Ashemeade had said that about the other house. Or had she? Which was this, a doll house in the Octagon House, or the Octagon House itself in some strange way?

The kitchen door, on the other hand, was standing ajar and Lorrie took that for an invitation. She came into warmth and good smells, and a feeling this was a good place to be. There was a big black pot on the range and from it came a soft bubbling noise. Lorrie sniffed the odor of fresh bread, and an even more mouth-watering spicy smell. On the table were all the things laid out to make a pie—a rolling pin, a waiting plate, a jug, some butter in a dish, a bowl with flour in it. And a pan of apples stood ready for the slicing knife. But where were the boy and girl? Or the cook who must have been busy here?

Lorrie looked around, knowing once more the feeling that someone had just stepped from the room as she entered. There was another door, but it was shut, and when she went to it, it was as tightly closed against her as Miss Ashemeade's had been.

So, only the kitchen and the back wall were open to her.

Lorrie moved slowly around the room. There was a big, polished brass pan hanging on the wall and it was almost as good as a mirror. She saw a reflection in it and stopped short to view herself. Of course she knew she was wearing the long skirt, which seemed fit and proper for riding here (where was *here?*), but now she saw other changes in Lorrie Mallard. Of course, she still had black hair and greeny eyes. But that hair was tied in a tight, turned-up, half bun at the back of her neck, and she had on a hat with a wide, curly brim and a soft feather drooping in the back. And instead of a zippered windbreaker she had worn outdoors a couple of hours ago, she now had a brown jacket, tight fitting and trimmed across the chest with rows of red braid, buttoned from her chin to her waist. She looked so different she could only stand and stare at that rather murky reflection.

She was Lorrie Mallard, Lorrie repeated to herself, Lorrie Mallard, eleven and a half years old. She lived with Aunt Margaret in the Ashton Arms apartment and she was in the sixth grade, the last year at Fermont School—that was the truth.

A sound broke through Lorrie's absorption and she turned around. Something outside the window—surely she had seen movement there! Quickly Lorrie hurried around the table. My, how dark it was getting! A bad storm—no, it must be night! That could not be true, it was only the middle of the afternoon. But Lorrie had to believe it was almost night now.

The pot continued to bubble comfortably, but no one came to see how it was doing. Once more Lorrie went to try the other door of the kitchen, to find it as firmly fixed as ever. As she stood by it she again heard that sound. There was a tall cabinet here and it was dark in this corner. Lorrie pressed back against the door and watched the far window.

There *was* a shadow there! She could see it against the small panes of glass. Now—that sound—the window was rising a little at a time.

Suddenly Lorrie crouched at the end of the cupboard. She did not know why she went into hiding, only that she was afraid and excited, and wanted to see without being seen.

For what seemed a long time to Lorrie nothing happened, except that the window was now open. Then a pair of hands gripped the sill, and behind them Lorrie made out a hunched outline that could be head and shoulders. Someone was climbing in!

It was darker in the kitchen than it had been when she had first entered. But there was a lamp on the table near the range. And, though its circle of light did not reach all the way to the window, Lorrie made out the figure huddled on the floor directly below the sill.

A boy! He had bare feet protruding below a pair of patched trousers all ragged at the ends. His hands and arms were bare almost to the elbow, and his shirt sleeves were tattered. There was no collar on the shirt, only a band fastened with a ragged strip of cloth. When he moved, it sprung open farther down his chest and Lorrie could see bare skin there also. He must not have anything on under that shirt, in spite of the cold.

His hair was an uncombed, unclipped mop that kept falling forward over his eyes, so that he was constantly raising his hand to push it back. And his face was very dirty. Around one of his eyes skin was puffed and dark and there was a greenish-blue bruise on the side of his jaw. Except to brush the hair out of his eyes, he had not moved since he dropped over the sill into the kitchen.

Now his head turned from side to side as he looked around the room. Lorrie thought he must be listening as well as looking, for now and then he stiffened and was still for a moment or two as if he could hear what she did not.

Then he got to his feet. He was very thin, his

arms so bony and his waist—where his trousers were belted with a piece of rope—so flat that Lorrie thought he certainly had not had enough to eat for a long time. He reached the side of the big table in a single stride and grabbed at the apples, putting them one after another into the front of his shirt where they made lumps under the grimy material.

The bowl emptied, he made for the half-open door of the range. His hand went to jerk the door farther open. Then he cried out softly and held his fingers to his mouth, but kept turning his head as if in search of something. He took up a poker and reached within the oven, pulling the bread pan forward, and then a second pan from which came the spicy smell. As those reached the door the boy hesitated. To pull them farther would dump them on the floor and apparently they were too hot to hold in his hands.

Again he looked around for a tool and caught a towel from a wall hook. With the towel wrapped around his already singed fingers, he brought the pans to the top of the stove before he snatched the red-and-white-checked cloth from a smaller table. He dumped into it the loaf of bread and the sheet of gingerbread, digging the latter out of its pan in great broken hunks. His head went up and he looked to the hall door. Jerking the cloth into the bag, he made for the window through which he had come, bundled out his loot first, and dropped after it into the night. The window slid down and Lorrie was alone.

She listened. Whatever the boy must have heard, or thought he had heard, she could not. But she wanted to know more— Why had he come to steal food? That was somehow important. Though she crossed to the window she could see nothing. But the window slid up smoothly at her pull. Without stopping to think, Lorrie followed the boy, climbing up to drop to the ground behind a bush. Now she could hear crackling off to her right, around the next angle of the house. Holding up the long skirt of her riding habit, she followed as fast as she could.

There was a brush screen close to the house as far as the next angle. Now she must be directly below that hidden, closed-in space, because before her was the window of the room with the painted floor. And from it came a beam of light.

Dark as it was, Lorrie discovered that she was able to follow the scurrying shadow as it flitted from one bush to another. Now it was heading for the fence. The bedroom windows were above, but there were no lights there. Lorrie glanced back and up at the house. On the second floor was a pale gleam in one window, as if a single candle was not too far away, but the rest was dark.

There was a swaying of bushes and Lorrie saw a black figure climb over the fence. She began to run for the gate, but to climb in this long skirt was out of the question. She came to the mounting block. And for a moment she was daunted, for the white horse was gone. Then she heard a noise to her left, and, gathering up her skirt with both hands, keeping to the pools of the shadows, she moved to where the boy had gone over the fence.

He was still keeping to cover. Then behind her she heard a faint creak and she stood still. Someone else was using the gate, a figure not much taller than she. Who?

Lorrie was undecided. If she stayed where she was she would lose the boy. If she kept on with the unknown behind her—Lorrie did not like the idea of being followed. And that other moved as carefully among the shadows as she was doing, as if dreading discovery.

She began to advance in a crabwise fashion, trying to watch both directions at once, which could not be done as she soon discovered. This was not Ash Street but a gravel road, bordered on both sides by trees and bushes. Shortly the gravel disappeared, leaving only hard-packed dirt.

The one behind her made a sudden dart forward, which brought her level with Lorrie. For it was a girl, a girl who could not have been much older than Lorrie herself. She wore a long, hooded cloak, but the hood was pushed back far enough so Lorrie could see her face. The newcomer passed within hand's distance of Lorrie without looking, as if indeed Lorrie were not there. She ran lightly after the boy.

Lorrie followed. There was a stream with a wooden bridge over it. But the girl from the house did not cross that. Instead she stood very still, her head bent to one side as if she were listening. Lorrie listened too—

She could hear the very faint rippling of the water below. But there was another sound also —someone was crying. And someone else was talking, a murmur that rose and fell but never quite drowned out the crying. To Lorrie's surprise the girl turned her head and now her eyes looked directly into Lorrie's. She did not seem in the least amazed, but as if she had known all along that Lorrie was there. And also as if, Lorrie thought, they were sharing this adventure.

Her finger was at her lips as she nodded sharply at the bridge from under which that crying came. Lorrie understood. She remained where she was, but the other girl crept forward very softly, drawing her cloak about her as if she did not want it to catch on any of the bushes or dried weeds.

The sound of talking below stopped, but the crying, now a very weak whimper, continued. Then, so suddenly Lorrie cried out, a black shadow rose from the weeds and threw itself at the girl. There was a struggle and she fell, the shadow trying to hold her down. Only she pulled free, leaving her cloak half torn off. Her hair tumbled loosely about her face and she raised her hands to push it back.

"Don't be afraid," she said.

"I ain't! Not of no girl, anyway." It was a hoarse boy's voice that answered. "What you doin', sneakin' up on—"

The girl gave her cloak a twitch, settling it smoothly about her shoulders again.

"You are from Canal Town." It was a statement, not a question this time.

"We ain't nobody, missy. You gets yourself outta here afore you gits into trouble."

"Phin? Where are you, Phin?" The whimpering had become a wail, and in it was a fear so strong Lorrie shivered in sympathy.

The boy moved, but the girl from the house was quicker. She slipped down the bank, under the overhang of the bridge. The boy scrambled after her, and now Lorrie dared go nearer.

"I am Lotta Ashemeade." That was the girl from the house, her voice calm. "You are afraid of something, bad afraid, aren't you?"

"Matt." There was a gulping sound. "Mat Mahoney. Dada died, and Matt, he says I must go to th' poor farm—"

"Close your trap, Phebe, close it tight! You want to be walked there straight off?"

"Stop it!" Lotta ordered. "You want to scare her to death, boy? She doesn't have to be afraid of me. Phebe, there's no reason to be afraid. Nobody's going to find you."

"No?" The boy again. "An' how kin you promise that, missy? You gotta army maybe to slow up Matt? Cause it'll take about that to stop him."

83

In answer the wail broke out louder than ever.

"I said to stop it!" There was authority in Lotta's voice and the wail became a whimper. "Come on, Phebe."

"An jus' where're you thinkin' of takin' her, missy? Back to that big ol' house of your'n? Keep her there an' send for Matt. Or maybe, her bein' an orphan, send her to th' pore farm yourself?"

"She's cold and she's wet and she's hungry. Oh, I know you got food out of our kitchen, for her. But see how she's shivering and she hasn't even a shawl. If she stays here tonight she'll be sick before morning."

"So—she ain't stayin'."

"How far do you think you can take her now?"

"What's it to you, anyhow? We're from Canal Town, we ain't big house folks. I'll do for Phebe, never no mind from you, missy. Come on, Phebe, we'll jus' move on a bit."

"Phin, I can't. My foot hurts so. I jus' can't! You—maybe you better run for it. Matt, he said he'd take th' horse whip to you, 'member? Oh, Phin, you jus' cut along. Missy, Matt he wants Phin to work for him. Only Phin, he thought we might jus' find some movers goin' west and maybe hide in a wagon—or somethin'."

"Spill it all now, will you, girl? Anyway, I has nowheres to go without you, Phebe. I keeps my promises. Ain't I always?"

"Then if you want Phebe to be safe, you'll come with me."

"An' why, missy? Why would you care?"

"I do."

She did, Lorrie knew that for the truth. Perhaps the boy recognized it also.

"Please, Phin."

"All right. Maybe I believe her, but there's other folks in that there ol' house an' they maybe ain't feelin' th' same way. Specially as how I helped myself pretty free to some o' their vittles a short while back."

"No one needs to know about you and Phebe. You'll be safe."

"What'd you mean, missy? You gonna fix us so no one kin see us, like we is ghosts or somethin' like?"

"Not that, Phin," Lotta answered. "But I do know of a safe place, at least for tonight. And it is warmer and dryer than under this bridge."

"Phin?" There was a pleading note in Phebe's voice.

"It ain't safe, I tell you."

"Please, Phin. She says it is. An'—an' I believe her, Phin."

" 'Cause you want to!" he flared up. " 'Cause you're cold an' hungry an' you want to! Ain't I told you a hundred times, it don't do no one any good to believe nothin' ner nobody?"

"I do her, Phin, somehow I do."

"All right. But I don't! You hear that, missy?

85

I don't believe, an' I'll be watchin' for any tricks."

"Fair enough. Now help me, Phin."

They came down the road again, Lotta, with her arm around a much smaller girl wearing a torn dress and with feet as bare as Phin's. She limped along slowly, though Phin and Lotta supported her more and more as they reached the gate. Again they made the journey around the house. This time they did not go as far as the kitchen, but instead to the window of the doll-house room.

Lorrie heard them whispering together and then saw Phin push at the window. When he had it open he helped Lotta over the sill, and a moment later they had boosted Phebe through. Lorrie moved in closer. She could see them all inside. Phebe was squatting on the floor as if she did not have the strength to stand, and Phin was staring about him warily, a scowl on his face, as if he believed he was in a trap.

Lotta had gone to the side by the window, out of Lorrie's sight. Then Phin exclaimed aloud in surprise.

"What's that there? A cupboard?"

"Bigger than a cupboard," Lotta answered him. "It's a safe hiding place for now."

He strode forward, also to disappear from Lorrie's sight.

"A trap—maybe jus' a trap—" She could still hear his voice.

"Please." Phebe raised her head to look at

Lotta. "I don't believe it, I don't believe you is goin' to send us back, missy. We ain't no kin to Matt. Jus' like Phin's no real kinfolk to me neither. Only he stood up to Matt when I got coughin' sick an' the shakes. An' Matt, he beat up Phin 'cause he traded some corn for medicine. Then Matt says he'd see I go to the pore farm. An' Phin says never, no to that an' we'd run. But we ain't far away and Matt he'll be after Phin does he stay here." She coughed, her thin body shaking with the effort.

Phin stepped back where Lorrie could see him again. "You ain't got th' little sense you was borned with, Phebe. Little missy here, she ain't a-carin' 'bout all that. Maybe Matt's got a poster out on me—Phineas McLean—ten shillin's reward—or th' like, but that ain't sayin' as how he'll ever lay his belt on me agin. 'Less missy here talks."

Lotta was at the door of the room. "If you truly believe that, Phineas McLean, you can go. The window's open." She gave him a long look and Phin made a gesture to push away his overgrown forelock but did not answer her. Then Lotta went out.

"Phin," Phebe choked out between coughs. "Phin, you'se always bin powerful good t' me. If you think Matt'll git you, you'd better go. Only I don't believe it—I don't. I think she's tellin' it true, we'll be safe here. I feel good, real good, right here. I truly, truly do, Phin!"

Once more he pushed back his hair, then he dropped on his knees beside Phebe and threw his arm about her shoulders.

"I ain't goin', girl. Leastwise, not tonight."

"Phin, don't you feel it, too? That this be a safe place?"

He was looking around, a rather puzzled expression on his bruised face.

"Maybe you is right, Phebe. Only it's right hard to believe in any place bein' safe for the likes of us—Canal Town trash, as they is always so quick to sing out."

"This is." Lotta was back. Across her arm was a quilt and a thick blanket. She nodded to the portion of the room Lorrie could not see. "Take these. And you had better get in there for now. I'll come when it is safe. And here—" Phin had taken the coverings from her, now Lotta picked up the tablecloth bag Lorrie had watched him fill. "Take this with you, I'll bring more later."

Wind was rising in the trees, the light in the room winked out . . . . Sunlight lay in a bar across the floor and in it lay Sabina asleep. Lorrie was not crouched down outside the window but she sat on the floor beside the doll house. Once more the side of the house hung a little open. She drew it the rest of the way to look into that small space with no proper door. It was empty.

In the kitchen the two dolls stood just as she had posed them. Carefully she took them out, knowing now who they were. Phineas McLean, no longer dirty, ragged, bruised—but she supposed that a doll would not look that way. His clothes were neat and whole, maybe this was meant to be Phineas truly safe and happy.

And Lotta—but no, this other doll did not have Lotta's features. This was Phebe, plumper, much happier looking. So maybe the house had welcomed them and continued to be their home. Why she thought that, Lorrie did not know.

She laid them back in their drawer and closed it. There was a click. The key on the chain—it was gone! When she tried the door again it was locked.

Phineas and Phebe were gone and the house— Now that she looked again Lorrie saw that the side of the house was once more tightly closed. Though she searched carefully for the latch, she could not find it.

Sabina awoke, yawned, got to her feet, stretched first front legs and then hind legs, and trotted to the door. More slowly Lorrie followed her, looking back once more at the baffling doll house.

A Collar for Sabina

"HEY, Canuck—"

Lorrie had paused at the mouth of the alley to take a tighter grip on the dress box. It was hard to manage that and her book bag too. Aunt Margaret had wanted to drive her to school this morning, but the car would not start. And Lorrie would have to hurry if she was going to get there in time.

It was just her luck that Jimmy and his gang were also late. Of course, maybe she could take refuge in the yard of Octagon House. She was somehow sure Jimmy would not follow her there. But such a detour would make her really tardy.

"Canuck, walks like a duck!"

Lorrie held the box tighter. It had her Puritan dress in it, and she had sewed a lot of that herself. Aunt Margaret had been surprised at how well she could do it. And Lorrie had pressed it and folded it neatly. She must not let it get wrinkled now.

"Canuck——"

Lorrie stared ahead. She was not going to run and let them chase her all the way to school. Boys——mean old boys!

She glanced to the house on her right. If only Hallie would come down to the back gate now. But every window was blank; it might have been deserted. Only——just looking at it——

What had Phin said? "Canal trash as they is so quick to sing out." Lorrie did not know why that flashed into her mind now. But for a moment it was almost as if she could see Phineas McLean pushing back his hair to glare at Lotta Ashemeade. She could hear Lotta's calm voice, see her refused-to-be-frightened face when she answered him. Why, just a moment ago Lorrie had been ready to run to the house for safety herself.

"Canuck—— What've you got in your box, Canuck? Give us a look."

Lorrie swung around.

Jimmy, yes, and Stan, and Rob Lockner. Jimmy in the lead as always, and grinning. For a moment Lorrie was afraid, so afraid that she thought she could not talk past the dryness in her mouth and throat. Then she thought of Lotta

91

and Phineas, and Phebe who had so much worse to fear.

"My dress for the play." Lorrie hoped her voice did not shake as much as she thought it did. "Where's your Indian suit, Jimmy? You certainly got a lot of feathers for your headband."

"He sure did," Rob Lockner broke in. "Know what he did? His uncle knows a man down at the zoo, and the birds there, they lose feathers. So he got real eagle feathers, didn't you, Jimmy?"

"Sure. That's what Indians wore, eagle feathers," Jimmy answered, but he was looking at Lorrie oddly, as if before his eyes she had turned into something quite different.

"The zoo." Lorrie did not have to pretend interest now. "I've never been there."

"Me, I go 'bout every Sunday," Jimmy returned. "My uncle, he got me a chance to see the baby tiger last year. They keep the baby animals in a different place, see, and you have to look at them through a window. But if you know somebody there they'll let you. This year they got a black leopard cub and two lions. I haven't seen them yet, but I'm going to." Jimmy's teasing grin was gone, he was talking eagerly. "They're just like kittens."

Kittens! For a moment Lorrie had a fleeting memory of Jimmy hunting Sabina through the tangled grass. She gripped her box more firmly and made herself walk at an even pace. Jimmy fell into step with her.

"You ought to see the snakes," he continued. "They got one as long as this alley."

"Aw, it's not that big," protested Stan.

Jimmy turned on him. "You say I don't know what I'm talking about?"

Stan shrugged and was quiet. But Jimmy continued, "And the alligator, you ought to see him! I had a chance to have an alligator once. My uncle was in Florida and he was going to send me one, a baby one. Only Mom said we didn't have any place to keep it."

"Boy, you know what I'd like to have?" Rob broke in. "A horse, that's what. Gee, I'd like to have one just like they used to keep in that stable over there."

"Hey, you know what's still in there?" Stan pointed back to the tumble-down carriage house. "There's a sled, only its for horses to pull. Neat, eh? Be fun to ride like that."

"It is," Lorrie agreed.

"How do you know?" Jimmy demanded.

"It used to snow a lot in Hampstead and there was a sleigh at school. We had sleigh rides sometimes."

"That true? A real sleigh with horses?" Jimmy sounded skeptical.

"Yes. It was old but they kept it fixed up and people used to rent it sometimes for parties. You'd ride out in it to the lake to go skating."

"Ice skating?" asked Rob. "You ice skate, Lorrie?"

" 'Most everyone did. I was learning figure skating." She thought that that was just one more thing she had lost.

"Hey"—Stan pushed up level with Jimmy and Lorrie—"there's the ice rink down by Fulsome. They let kids in Saturday mornings. Last year Mr. Stewart talked about it in gym, said we might like to learn. We saw a picure about the Olympic skaters in assembly. They sure were neat!"

"It's hard to learn the fancy things," Lorrie answered. "There was a girl at Miss Logan's, she was good. But she had been skating since she was five and she practiced all the time. I guess you have to, if you want to be good."

"We went to the Ice Follies last spring," Rob volunteered. "They had this guy, he was dressed up like a bear, see, and he chased another guy who was a hunter all around. Gee, it sure was funny!"

"Dad said he was going to get us tickets this year," Jimmy cut in.

They had reached the school crossing, and Lorrie looked to the clock over the main door.

"We're going to be late."

Jimmy followed her gaze. "Not if we zoom—"

"Yah, yah! I'm a Purple Hornet, zoom, zoom, zoom!" yelled Stan.

"Me, I'm riding the fastest horse on earth! Get going, Paint!" Rob took out after Stan.

"Gimme that. You're going to have to run, Canuck!" Jimmy grabbed at Lorrie's book bag.

They ran for the door as the clock boomed out and they heard the ring of the warning bell. And Lorrie was not sure how it happened that she entered the school with Jimmy Purvis carrying her book bag, somehow not minding at all that he had called her Canuck as he pounded along beside her.

The Thanksgiving weekend was exciting for Lorrie because Aunt Margaret had two whole days free. They went shopping for a new best dress for Lorrie, and had lunch in the big restaurant at the very top of Bamber's store, from which you could see all over the city. Aunt Margaret had gone out with her on the terrace to look down at the buildings and streets that made up Ashton.

"There will be some changes next year," Aunt Margaret said. "The new thruway will pass not far from us, you know. The world moves fast nowadays, Lorrie. See, down there—" She pointed to a narrow strip leading into the river. "That is all that is left of the old canal. And only a little more than a hundred years ago travel on that was as exciting as travel by jet plane is for us today. Why, Ashton was built because of the junction with the river."

"Where was Canal Town?" asked Lorrie suddenly.

Aunt Margaret looked surprised. "Canal Town? I never heard of that, Lorrie. Where did you hear it mentioned?"

"At Octagon House." Lorrie was alert to her mistake. She did not know why, but she was sure that her adventure with Phineas and Phebe was something to be kept to herself. Why, she had not even spoken of it when she had gone back to join Miss Ashemeade on the afternoon when it happened. Yet of one thing she was sure—Miss Ashemeade had somehow known all of what had happened to her.

"Yes, Octagon House," Aunt Margaret said slowly. "It is a pity."

"What is a pity?"

"They have not quite decided on the linkup with the thruway, but they believe it will cross the land on which Octagon House stands."

Lorrie held hard to the terrace railing.

"They—they couldn't take the house—pull it down—could they?" She stared out over the city, trying to see the house. But, of course, it was too far away.

"Let us hope not," answered Aunt Margaret. "Now it is cold here, isn't it? And I want to look at those blouses on sale, if we can get near enough to the counter. Most of Ashton appears to be doing their Christmas shopping this weekend."

Christmas—she wanted to get Grandmother's gift today. Aunt Margaret said it must be mailed this coming week. For a moment Lorrie forgot the threat against Octagon House.

"Lorrie," Aunt Margaret said that evening. "Do you suppose that Miss Ashemeade would care if I asked to see some of her needlework? You've talked so much about it that you've made me curious. Would you take a note over for me tomorrow?"

Lorrie was surprised at her own feelings. There was no reason in the world why Aunt Margaret would not want to see all the treasures in the red room. But—but it was as if her going there spoiled something—what? Lorrie could not say, and she knew, she told herself, she was being silly.

"All right." She hoped her voice did not sound grudging.

She wrapped Grandmother's scarf ready for mailing. Then she spread out all Aunt Margaret's gift paper and examined it piece by piece. There was one sheet she set aside. The background was green, not quite the green of Miss Ashemeade's dress, but close to it. And the pattern over that was a big golden-purple-green of peacock feathers. Lorrie was entranced by it. There was gold ribbon that was perfect against it. She slid the white handkerchief box onto it and turned the paper up and around with all the care she could. Then the ribbon was looped, as Aunt Margaret had shown her, in a special bow. Yes, it looked almost as pretty as she had hoped. And the handkerchief —she had been lucky to find it among all the rest—so many ladies had been picking and pulling them around. But this was white and it had a narrow border of lace with a big A in the

corner. Lorrie had added a little wreath about
that with her best stitches.

She went to put it away in the drawer that
was kept for Christmas. There was one other
thing among those already there. She had finished
it last week and she hoped Aunt Margaret would
like it, though now she wondered. In Octagon
House when she had made it, it looked pretty
and amusing. But in this room would a plump
red-velvet heart pincushion with a white lace
frill fit? Aunt Margaret liked old-fashioned
things though. And Lorrie had a bottle of her
favorite cologne, too.

Octagon House—and the thruway. Lorrie went
back to the living room.

"When will they know?"

Aunt Margaret looked up from her book.
"Know what, Chick?"

"Know about Octagon House?"

"There will be a meeting late in January, I
believe. All the people whose property will be
affected will have a chance to meet with the
Commission."

Lorrie wondered if Miss Ashemeade knew.
Could she go to the meeting? Twice only had
Lorrie seen her walk. Both times she had moved
very slowly, one hand on Hallie's shoulder, the
other on a gold-headed cane. She never went
out of the house, Lorrie knew. Once a week a
boy came up from Theobald's grocery and got
a list from Hallie. Lorrie herself had taken that

list in when the boy had the flu. Hallie did not go out either. So what would happen if Miss Ashemeade could not go to that meeting and protest about Octagon House's being torn down?

"Miss Ashmeade's lame, she can't walk very much." Lorrie put her fear into words. "What if she can't go to the meeting?"

"She may send a lawyer, Lorrie. Most of the people will have lawyers to represent them."

Lorrie sighed. She hoped that was true. But tomorrow she would ask Miss Ashemeade, tell her about the need for a lawyer to go to the meeting.

Only, when she was settled by Miss Ashemeade the following afternoon, her workbox open beside her and Miss Ashemeade's regiment of needles all waiting to have their gaping eyes filled, Lorrie somehow found it hard to begin.

"You are unhappy." Miss Ashemeade adjusted the embroidery frame. It was dark outside, grayish, but she had candelabras, each bearing four candles, perched on high candle stands to either side. "Has Jimmy Purvis been a problem again?"

Lorrie drew the soft strand of cream wool through the needle and stuck it carefully on the side of the canvas.

"He still calls me Canuck, but I don't care any more."

"So?" Miss Ashemeade smiled. " 'Sticks and stones may break my bones, but names will never hurt me.' Is that it, Lorrie?"

99

"Not exactly." Lorrie added a needle with a burden of pearl-pink to the first. "Only, I think he does not mean it the same way. He likes to talk a lot."

"And you do not find it hard to listen? When he's such a mean and hateful person?"

Lorrie carefully chose a strand of wool of rose color. "Maybe—maybe he isn't so mean and hateful any more. He's changed."

"Or you know him better and do not see only the outer covering. Things do change, Lorrie, and sometimes for the better. One time, many years ago, some people lived just a little way from here. The men had come to work on the canal. But they had come from another country so they spoke differently, they went to another kind of church than the one in the village. Because they felt so different they kept to themselves. And the village people did not welcome any of them who tried to be friends. Then there was often trouble—fighting.

"Some of these men later brought their families here because there was a famine in their own country and nothing left for them there. Others had wives from other parts of this land. But when they came here to live there was ill feeling. Because they did not know each other a wall grew higher and higher, until both the canal people and the village would believe any sort of evil of the other."

Lorrie put another cream-threaded needle into

the side of the frame. "You're talking about Phebe and Phineas, aren't you, Miss Ashemeade?"

"Phebe and Phineas, and many others like them. Though they did not know it, the night they came here Phebe and Phineas made the first small break in that wall. They trusted someone on the other side. But it meant changes on both sides. People had to learn not to look for what they feared to see."

Lorrie unwound a strand of coral wool, measured the proper length, and cut it with small scissors fashioned in stork shape, the long bill being the sharp blades.

"You mean—I was afraid of Jimmy, so I saw him that way. But why did he—"

"Begin to call you Canuck and chase you? Well, perhaps Jimmy thought it a joke at first and if you had laughed, that would have been the end of it. Then, as some people are very like to do, he found he enjoyed chasing you because you ran, or showed that you disliked and feared him. When you began to treat him as if you were not afraid, he stopped hunting you. You may not want Jimmy for a close friend, that is true. But I do not believe you dislike him so much."

"No, I don't." Lorrie chose a reel of golden tan. "Miss Ashemeade, what happened to Phineas and Phebe afterward?"

There was such a long moment of silence that Lorrie looked up in surprise, the needle in one hand, the end of the wool in the other. Miss

Ashemeade was no longer smiling. Instead she was looking at something she had taken out of the sewing table, turning it around between her fingers. It was the box that held the golden needles.

"They made a choice, Lorrie, and thereafter they lived by it. Some can be so hurt by the world that they choose to turn their backs upon it. My, look at the snow!"

Lorrie turned to the window. Flakes were whirling down, to be seen in the crack between the lace edges of the curtains. There was a soft mew and Sabina leaped to the sill, to stand on her hind legs, patting the panes furiously, trying to get at those fluttering crystals.

"No more needles, Lorrie," Miss Ashemeade said. "I think there is other work to be done this afternoon. Sabina is very good at reminding one."

Lorrie helped her set away the frame and then watched curiously as Miss Ashemeade got to her feet with difficulty. She moved forward impulsively and Miss Ashemeade accepted her help, putting her hand on Lorrie's shoulder as she had on Hallie's arm.

They began a slow progress to the big table on which lay the materials, the various pieces of half-finished mending work Miss Ashemeade kept at hand. She did not pause by the lace, or by the moth-holed tapestry, or by the beautiful coat of silk that had the wonderful birds embroidered on it (and that Miss Ashemeade said had been made

102

a very long time ago in China for an emperor to wear). Instead they came to the far end of the table where there were no pieces waiting for repair, but rather rolls of cloth and ribbon, each neatly packaged and tied with leftover twists of wool. Miss Ashemeade stood there for what seemed to Lorrie a very long moment. And then she said:

"That red-velvet ribbon, Lorrie, there next to the blue. That is what I need."

The velvet was very thick, but silky feeling. And the color was that of the garnets Miss Ashemeade wore. Once it was in Lorrie's hand, the old lady made a slow progress back to her chair. And when she was again seated she kept the roll of ribbon on her lap while she examined intently all the spools and reels housed in the compartments of the table top. Finally she lifted out a spindle of black wood. Wound about it was a glistening thread, as brightly silver, Lorrie thought, as the trimming of a Christmas tree she had seen in Bamber's.

Then Miss Ashemeade took up a little box from another compartment and when she moved it, there was a faint tinkling sound.

"Merrow!" Sabina jumped from the window sill, came in two leaps to Miss Ashemeade's side, and now stood on her hind legs, her eyes fixed upon the box that rang so.

Miss Ashemeade lifted the lid.

"Bells!" Lorrie had been as curious as Sabina.

"Bells," agreed Miss Ashemeade. She took out one about as big as the nail on her little finger and shook it gently. The tinkle was faint, but pretty. There were bells even smaller, but none larger. "Do you approve, Sabina?" Miss Ashemeade held the velvet ribbon in one hand, the bell box in the other, for the kitten to see and sniff.

It seemed to Lorrie that Sabina studied them carefully, as if they had a meaning for her.

"Merrow!" Sabina rubbed her head against Miss Ashemeade's hand, and then was back at the window again with a whisk of her tail.

Miss Ashemeade picked up the box that held the golden needles. As she opened it she spoke to Lorrie.

"My dear, will you play the music box for us?"

The music box had its own table. It was of polished, dark red wood, and its lid was bordered with small white blocks of ivory. You pressed a small lever after you raised the lid, and the music came. Like the bells it was a soft, tinkling music, but Lorrie loved it. She started it now and the tune filled the room.

"Quite right and proper—the 'Magic Flute,'" said Miss Ashemeade. "This is an afternoon for magic, Lorrie. Some days are, some days are not."

"Because it is snowing? I never thought of snow being magic."

"Much of the magic of this world does not seem to exist just because we are too blind, or too busy to look for it, Lorrie. Blindness and unbelief, those are the two foes of magic. To see and to believe—those who do have many gates to enter, if they choose."

She measured out the velvet ribbon, doubling it into two thicknesses when she had the length she wished. Then she cut off a piece of the silver thread.

"Do you want me to thread it?" offered Lorrie.

Miss Ashemeade shook her head. "Not this thread, not this needle, Lorrie. This can only be my doing at this time."

It was one of the golden needles she used. The thread went in smoothly and she began to stitch the ribbon double. Lorrie, so used to seeing her at the exacting work on tapestry or lace, had never watched Miss Ashemeade sew so swiftly. It was not a straight hemming stitch either, for the needle worked a pattern along the edge. Also, Lorrie thought, the gold needle was brighter in the candlelight than the silver ones, flashing in and out, so sometimes it appeared as if Miss Ashemeade was not using a needle at all, but a splinter of light.

Lorrie brought out her own sewing. This was for Christmas and she had been happy with it. But now that she looked at the simple design of white flowers across the red apron, she was not satisfied. The flowers seemed coarse and big, and she was not certain the pattern was even straight.

In the room the music box played and Miss

Ashemeade's needle flashed in and out. Sabina gave up trying to reach the snowflakes and came back to sprawl out on the hearthrug. All at once, Lorrie, in spite of her misgivings about the apron, was happy. She was safe—safe—safe— There was warmth here, and happiness, and all the good one could wish for. Outside lay cold and dark, but here was warmth and light—

It was moments before she realized that the music box had stopped. But there was still a murmur of sound and it was Miss Ashemeade singing. Lorrie could hear what she thought were words, but she could not understand them. The song went on and on and the needle flew. Now every once in a while Miss Ashemeade chose a bell from the box, using only the smaller ones, and fastened it to the velvet strip to fringe it, and their tinkling was a part of the song Lorrie could not understand.

Lorrie's own stitches seemed to come faster and easier too, and her thread did not tangle. And somehow she found she was putting in her needle and drawing it out in time to certain repeated notes of the song. When she did it that way, her needle flashed almost as quickly as Miss Ashemeade's. She was humming and, though she did not know the words, she could follow the tune.

"Ahh—"

Lorrie started, pricking her finger on her needle.

Miss Ashemeade held up the belled strip of velvet so Lorrie saw it plainly for the first time.

"A collar?" she asked.

"Just so, my dear, a collar. Sabina must have a Christmas gift also."

"But will she want to wear it—some cats—" Lorrie knew that much about cats.

"*Some* cats are not Sabina, she is a very special cat. As for collars, this one she will want to wear, when the time comes. And—it is four o'clock. Hallie has some gingerbread and Chinese tea. I think we would be refreshed by both."

The golden needle was gone, the case that held it back in its compartment. Miss Ashemeade rang her little bell. Then she smiled at Lorrie.

"It seems you have spent the afternoon profitably also, Lorrie. Only a stitch or two more and your apron is complete."

Lorrie was surprised when she looked at her work. She *had* done most of it! And it had seemed so easy too, once she had begun. She folded it carefully into the lower section of the workbox.

"Miss Ashemeade," she said slowly, "do you know a lawyer?"

"In my lifetime, Lorrie, I have known several. Why? Are you now at odds with the law?" Miss Ashemeade smiled as she closed her worktable.

"Because—Aunt Margaret said that there was going to be trouble about the thruway—that—that they might want to run it right here!"

Miss Ashemeade no longer smiled. Her hands rested quietly on the top of the table.

"There has been such talk."

"But Aunt Margaret said they are going to have another meeting to talk about it, and that the people who couldn't go to the meeting could have a lawyer speak for them."

"I believe that is so. And you are worried about me, Lorrie? Yes, I see that you are. Well, we shall see what we shall see. I am not defenseless, Lorrie, not entirely defenseless."

Now she was smiling again. "And, Lorrie, if you wish, please come to tea tomorrow. And"—she motioned to the tall desk standing in a darker corner of the room—"If you will bring me paper, pen, and ink, my dear, I shall write a note to your Aunt Margaret. I should very much like her to come also."

Lorrie went to get Miss Ashemeade what she wanted, but she hoped as she went that Miss Ashemeade was right, that she had a defense against the thruway. Because—because—Lorrie could not bear that thought. Not this house—this room—to be pulled all to pieces.

Octagon House
Keeps Christmas

THERE had been more snow during the night, and in the morning too, while they were in church. But in the afternoon, while Aunt Margaret and Lorrie had tea in Miss Ashemeade's warm red room, the sun came out and made thousands of sparkles across the drifts. Sabina sat before the fire and purred to herself, a song, Lorrie thought, not unlike the one Miss Ashemeade had sung when she worked on the collar.

She dropped down beside the kitten and stared into the flames, another world all red and yellow trees and—Sabina purred while the fire crackled gently to itself.

Aunt Margaret and Miss Ashemeade were examining the framed embroidery pictures and panels on the wall. That is, Aunt Margaret moved about, looking at them, asking questions that Miss Ashemeade answered from her chair. There were lots of candles, all lighted, as well as the sun at the windows, so one could see. Lorrie heard the excited note in Aunt Margaret's voice after she had made the circuit of the room and came back to sit down again by the window.

"—museum pieces!"

"Perhaps in this day and age. Much has been forgotten. But they were made for pleasure and with pride of talent. They were fashioned because the urge to do so was great."

"Carolinian stump work! And those needle-work engravings—the samplers! One reads of such things, but they are seldom to be seen. And the tapestries"—Aunt Margaret kept turning her head from side to side—"such needlepoint! It is fabulous. I have never seen such a complete collection—it must date back three hundred years —and such perfect condition!"

"Oh, thread and fabric wear through the dust of years. But there are precautions one may take, of course. I have reason to care for them since they give me pleasure and I do not go abroad nowadays. But all things pass with the years themselves. Perhaps the time will come when none shall care. And if there is no one to do so, then it is better such work vanish. But this is no day, with the sun bright and the snow all dia-monds, to think of that, is it?"

She rang her bell and nodded at Lorrie. "My dear, I think that perhaps you may help Hallie. Dear Hallie, her baking tins and mixing bowls are to her what my needles and threads are to me, and she so seldom has a chance to show her skills nowadays. I think she has, perhaps, as the saying goes, outdone herself today. Company for Sunday tea is a pleasure we have not had for a long time."

Lorrie went to the kitchen. She had peeped within it several times as she went through the hall on her other visits. But somehow she felt shy about entering without Hallie's invitation. Just as she never entered the red room without knocking and waiting for Miss Ashemeade to call, "Come." Now she stared about her with frank curiosity. Why, it was almost exactly the same as that kitchen where she had hidden to watch Phineas steal the bread and the gingerbread. Only this time there were no preparations of pie making on the table.

Instead there was a shining silver tray and on it a silver sugar bowl, a cream pitcher, and another rounded container in which teaspoons with flower-patterned handles stood upright. Hallie was at the big range, filling the silver teapot with water from a steaming kettle. She smiled at Lorrie sniffing the spicy odors that all at once made her sure she was hungry.

"Come to help, Mis' Lorrie? That's fine. Hallie hasn't got her four arms, or five hands, or a little fairy wand to push an' pull an' fly things 'round for her. You take that cloth now an' put it on the tea table. They's napkins with it, don't drop them, child. Then, if you'll came back, we'll git along with the rest."

Lorrie could hardly believe this was meant to be a tablecloth, it was such fine material and bordered with lace. But she followed Hallie's instructions and then trotted again across the triangle of hallway with the napkin-covered plates Hallie gave her.

"Hallie," Aunt Margaret observed, when those napkins were gathered up to show such numbers of small cakes, sandwiches, things Lorrie did not even know how to make, "you are an artist! These look far too good to eat."

Hallie laughed. "Now, Mis' Gerson, that's what they's made for, an' it gives me a pleasurin' to have a chance to keep my hand in a-makin' 'em all. Mis' Charlotta, she don't eat no more'n a bird."

"I don't believe you have ever watched a bird, Hallie," laughed Miss Ashemeade, "if you say that. They eat *all* the time when they can find sustenance. As one grows old the sharpness of one's senses is curtailed. Taste and smell are not what they once were, and then half the pleasure of food has fled. So Hallie is enjoying herself today, having a chance to cater to more appreciative and larger appetites than mine."

Sabina mewed loudly, pressing her small body

against Miss Ashemeade's wide folds of skirt. Though Miss Ashemeade's dress was made the same as the green one, today it was gray, with a wide collar of cobwebby lace lying on her shoulders. The ends of the lace hung to her waist. On her wrists were wide bracelets of black enamel with small pearl flowers set in wreaths on them. A big pin of the same workmanship, with a whole bouquet of seed pearls on it, fastened the collar.

Now one of the bracelets turned round and round as if it were made for a much plumper wrist, as Miss Ashemeade gently pulled her skirt from the claws Sabina was daring to lay in its folds.

"Not so, Sabina. You have tea, to be sure, but in the proper place. We have nothing here to interest small cats."

"Come on, Sabina." Hallie moved toward the door. "You's not forgotten."

Sabina scurried past Hallie, heading for the kitchen, and Miss Ashemeade laughed again. "Now there goes one who is certainly *not* unmindful of the pleasures of the table."

Later, when they were walking home in the early winter dusk, Aunt Margaret spoke suddenly:

"I felt as if I had been caught in a fairy tale when I was in that house. It has an enchantment, Lorrie. Time seems to stand still there—" Her voice trailed off as if she were thinking.

"They mustn't tear it down!" Lorrie voiced

113

the fear that had been with her at intervals since Aunt Margaret had first mentioned the thruway.

"We feel that, Lorrie. But in the name of progress more than one crime is committed nowadays. I wonder just who will rejoice when the last blade of grass is buried by concrete, when the last tree is brought down by a bulldozer, when the last wild thing is shot, or poisoned, or trapped. Lorrie—" again Aunt Margaret hesitated "—don't set your heart on saving Octagon House."

"But—but where would Miss Ashemeade and Hallie and Sabina go?"

Aunt Margaret shook her head and did not answer. After a moment Lorrie said angrily:

"I don't believe it! And I'm not going to think it will happen!"

"Please, Lorrie." Aunt Margaret looked at her anxiously. "Hope for what you wish, yes, but you must learn to accept disappointment. Learn all you can from Octagon House, because it has a great deal to offer one who has eyes to see. But it belongs to another day, when time itself moved slower. We believe we have mastered time in some ways, but when one opens one's hand to grasp a new thing, one has to let go of an old. Do you understand what I mean, Lorrie?"

"I think so. But I don't believe it is good to put that street through here!"

"Maybe we don't believe so, Lorrie, but you wouldn't find many to agree with us. Anyway, there is still the meeting and a chance the plan will not go through. In the meantime, Miss Ashemeade has invited us to spend the afternoon of Christmas Day with her."

"Really and truly?" Lorrie grabbed at Aunt Margaret's hand and squeezed it as tight as the mitten and glove covering their hands would allow. "Are we going?"

"Yes. She is being very kind, for she said I might bring the camera and take pictures of those wonderful needlework pieces. They can't ever be copied, such work is not possible today. But some of the patterns might be adapted. Though"—Aunt Margaret sighed—"for anyone who has seen the originals, copies will be sorry substitutes."

The days until Christmas might have dragged, except there was so much to do. Lorrie was one of the Holly Chorus at school for the Christmas Assembly and went about singing "Deck the halls with boughs of holly" until Aunt Margaret said that she had no objection to carols but they did seem to ooze out of the walls at this time of year and were hard to think by.

Then she produced tickets for a special Walt Disney movie downtown. And Lorrie asked Kathy and Rob Lockner, and Lizabeth Ross, who was beside her in the Holly Chorus, to go. They had lunch at Bamber's and after the movie a sundae at Walker's, with a trip through the Freeman toy shop at the end of the day.

"Gee, Lorrie, Miss Gerson, that was swell," Rob commented as they came upstairs.

"I loved it when the fairy turned them all into animals," Kathy said. "Thank you, Miss Gerson."

Lorrie agreed it had all been super. But back in the apartment she sat down in the first chair to take off her boots, and her face was sober.

"Too much show, or ice cream, or walking?" asked Aunt Margaret. "I will admit that pushing through crowds is rather trying."

Lorrie looked up. "You know," she spoke half accusingly. "Why—why wouldn't Kathy sit next to Lizabeth? She pushed me in ahead when I was being polite to let her in first. I think Lizabeth knew it too. She didn't talk much after that. It isn't fair! Lizabeth's nice, she's smart, and she's pretty. Kathy was mean."

"I don't think Kathy was being mean exactly," Aunt Margaret answered. "Kathy doesn't see things the way you do, Lorrie. For a long, long time there have been separations between people. That this is not right, we know now more and more. But when people stand apart and do not try to make friends, walls go up between them, and they believe all kinds of untrue things about the person on the other side of the wall. The less they know about a stranger, the more ready they are to believe that he is bad in one way or another.

"I don't believe that Kathy ever in her life

116

before spent an afternoon with Lizabeth or any little girl of another race or color. So she was feeling strange and did not know what to do, while Lizabeth drew back and did not try any more to be friendly after Kathy had snubbed her. Both of them had a chance to break down that wall a little, but neither made the attempt."

"But you tried to have them do it, didn't you, Aunt Margaret?" Lorrie set aside her boots. "That's why you had them look at the stuffed animals together."

"Yes. And I think that next time Kathy will wonder if Lizabeth isn't like her after all. They both liked the big fox and the baby owls. When they forgot themselves, they talked about those, remember?"

"Then you don't think that—that Lizabeth will be mad at me?"

"Not in the least. And now, I am just a tired old aunt. Do you think you can get me a bite of supper all by yourself as a good, kind, obedient niece should?"

"One supper coming right up!" Lorrie jumped to her feet. It was about Phineas and Phebe she thought as she looked into the freezer for inspiration. They had not had friends either. Miss Ashemeade had said they had stayed on at Octagon House. Odd—Lorrie paused between stove and table. She had never spoken to Aunt Margaret about the doll house. Yet that was a bigger treasure than all the pieces of embroidery.

No—the doll house was something else. When had it been made? There was no miniature of it inside the smaller house. That room had only the chair, the painting on the floor, the shelves with their bottles and books, some dried plants hanging in bundles along the walls, and also that secret place where Lotta had hidden Phineas and Phebe.

Lotta lived in the house. But who else did? Lotta was only a little girl, not much older than Lorrie. Did she have a father and mother? Brothers and sisters? Who had baked the bread and the gingerbread Phineas stole? Was the doll house itself made for the Lotta of long ago?

There were so many questions. But maybe Lorrie could find the answers to a few of them. Only—again Lorrie stopped to think—she did not want to see the doll house often. Lorrie wondered about that a little. The first time—then she had been exploring as Miss Ashemeade suggested. And when she had had the second adventure, Miss Ashemeade had sent her to find Sabina. She was sure that Miss Ashemeade knew both times about her visits back to that other time. Then, did Miss Ashemeade intend her to have those adventures. Why? And would she have any more?

Lorrie put down the butter dish she was carrying. She was not quite sure she wanted any more rides.

The school Christmas program was over and

vacation began. Christmas was on Saturday, but Aunt Margaret had to work until the Wednesday before. The Lockners were going away on Tuesday and Lorrie persuaded Mrs. Lockner that she had Christmas presents to finish and wanted to work on them at home. But she dutifully went there to lunch on Monday and helped Kathy wash dishes afterward.

The next morning the boy from the grocery brought a note from Octagon House. Miss Ashemeade wondered if Lorrie would like to help with Christmas decorations. Aunt Margaret agreed, and by ten Lorrie was tramping along the snow-covered brick walk around to the back door.

She shed her boots, ski pants, and jacket in the hall. Hallie came to the door of the kitchen with two big bowls in her hands. One was mounded with cranberries, the other had fluffy popcorn heaped high in it.

"You're jus' in good time, child, to save old Hallie a couple of steps an' a minute or two. You take this in."

The cranberries were raw, even if the corn was popped. Did Miss Ashemeade mean they were to eat them so? But without asking questions Lorrie took the bowls into the red room.

There had been changes there. The sewing table was moved back against the wall, the embroidery frame pushed beside it. Another small table stood beside Miss Ashemeade's chair, hold-

ing only her needle box, a pair of scissors, and
a very large spool of coarse white thread. On the
stool where Lorrie usually sat stood a box, its
lid thrown back, and out of that Miss Ashemeade
was taking small bundles of old, much creased
tissue paper and cotton.

"You are in good time, my dear. Now, do
you suppose you can move up that other table?
Put the bowls over here, then just set this box on
the floor. There, we are quite in order now. What
do you think of the tree?"

It stood there, bare and green and fragrant,
between the two windows. And it must have been
placed on a box now wrapped with green cloth,
for it was not a full-sized one. As if reading
Lorrie's thought, Miss Ashemeade shook her
head.

"We used to have a proper tree, tall enough
to top all heads. But I did not believe we could
manage to trim such a one now. We shall have
work enough to dress one this size."

She was pulling away the paper and cotton
wrappings from things she took from the box,
setting each with a gentle touch, as she freed it,
on the table Lorrie had moved close to her.
There was a row of tiny baskets, some with lids.
Next came walnut shells, gilded and fastened
half open so that one could peep inside. Lorrie
did, to discover that they cradled tiny, brightly
colored pictures of flowers, animals, boys and
girls. Then there were flat ornaments of card-

board, velvet-covered and edged with gold-and-silver paper lace, in the center of each a larger picture.

Miss Ashemeade held some a little longer than others, as if they brought her memories. One of these was a cage of fine golden wire, within it a bird fashioned of tiny shells. And there were more baskets, made of cloves strung on wire with a glass bead inset on every wire crossing.

"Oh, I had forgotten, almost I had forgotten." Miss Ashemeade held a small round box on her hand. "Look at this, Lorrie. When I was younger this was a dear treasure."

In the box was a set of four bowls, bowls so tiny Lorrie did not see how anyone could ever make them. But the greatest wonder was that in each of those minute bowls rested a silver spoon!

"So little!" marveled Lorrie.

"They are carved from cherry stones, my dear." Miss Ashemeade carefully set aside the box. "See, here are some similar carvings." She uncoiled a piece of thin cord. Fastened to it at intervals were baskets, only one or two as big as Lorrie's finger nail. "These, and these, are from cherry stones. And that—that is a hazel nut, and that an acorn. This is sturdy enough to hang on the tree. But the bowls—they are too easily lost."

"I never saw such things."

"No," Miss Ashemeade agreed, "perhaps you have not. You see, once people made all their own decorations. We did not have the fine glass pieces that were for sale. So we used our imagination and made our own pretty things."

"I like these better than the store things." Lorrie did not touch the peep-show walnut shells, the cord of nut baskets, or any of the treasures Miss Ashemeade had set out. She wanted to, but she did not quite dare.

"So do I, my dear. But then I have known them for a long, long time and old things grow into one's heart and memory until one cannot lose them, even when one can no longer do this." She picked up one of the walnuts and smiled down at it. Within a dove fluttered white wings above blue and pink flowers.

"Now." She put aside the walnut and picked up a needle case from the other table. "We shall need some long thread, Lorrie, as long as might go around the tree at least once."

Lorrie cut the thread and put it through the needle eyes. Miss Ashemeade took a cranberry and speared it neatly, drawing the thread through it. Three more cranberries went on and then a grain or two of popcorn before more berries.

"That is the way to do it," she said.

Eagerly Lorrie set to work with another needle. As they made the chains Miss Ashemeade told stories. They were Christmas stories and now and then she touched some ornament on the table as she spoke.

So many Christmases, all in this house. And

every one Miss Ashemeade spoke about as if she remembered it for herself. But to Lorrie that did not seem strange, though surely Miss Ashemeade could not be as old as that!

But though she talked of the house and the things in it, of how this or that was made or used, she never spoke of the people in the house. She only said "we did" this or that.

They had quite a pile of chains finished and all the cranberries were gone from the bowl when Hallie came in with a big tray that she set on one end of the long table.

"Here they all is, Mis' Charlotta. An' they turned out jus' fine."

"I see they did, Hallie. The red eyes for the mice were an inspiration! What do you think of Hallie's contribution to the tree, Lorrie?"

"This ain't all—" Hallie was already on her way back to the kitchen. "I has the candies for the baskets, an' the gingerbread—"

But Lorrie hardly heard her. She was too amazed by the tray on the table. Mice, three rows of white mice, all with red eyes, small pink cardboard ears, and string tails! And behind them another three rows of pink pigs!

"Sugar mice and pigs." Miss Ashemeade laughed. "They are good to eat, too, Lorrie. Hallie has always been a master hand at mice and pigs for the tree. We shall make some ribbon collars for them to hang by. That very narrow red-and-green ribbon over there ought to do.

123

And I think, I really think, Lorrie, you might test Hallie's proficiency by tasting one of each."

Lorrie selected a very plump pink pig and nibbled up its hind legs. It was sugary and good, so good the rest of the pig vanished very fast indeed. But she set the mouse aside to look at, determining to take him home to show Aunt Margaret.

While Miss Ashemeade measured and cut lengths of ribbon, Hallie brought in a second tray. There were gingerbread men wearing coats of white frosting, trousers of red, with currant eyes and squiggles of chocolate frosting for hair. And gingerbread ladies in their company with skirts striped red-and-white and blouses of white with red buttons. There were horses with frosting manes and tails, and half a dozen cats with frosting whiskers and eyes of bits of candied green cherry.

"Well, Hallie, these are the best yet!" Miss Ashemeade put aside the ribbon and leaned forward in her chair.

"I thought as how it should be, Mis' Charlotta —considerin'," Lorrie heard Hallie answer.

"Quite right, Hallie, quite right. I do not think we shall try to hang these, Lorrie. But we can set them about in the branches."

"I'll get the candies now, for the little baskets—" Hallies was gone again.

Lorrie continued to study the gingerbread

people. "I never saw anything like them. They're precious!"

"Very dashing, those gentlemen," Miss Ashemeade commented. "Quite the beaux. But the ladies, they look flighty to me. However, elegant, very elegant. They all have quite an air of high fashion, I would say."

"Here's the candies." Hallie came back with a third tray, even larger than the first two. And Lorrie quickly moved a pile of folded material to make a place for it on the table.

Just as the mice, pigs, and gingerbread company, here, too, works of art were set out. Tiny sugar flowers, miniature chocolate drops, a wealth of little things, too many for Lorrie to see all at once.

Miss Ashemeade pulled toward her some of the small baskets.

"They go into these, Lorrie. Let me see now, it was always the peppermint drops in the green baskets, and the chocolates in the white and the sugar flowers in the red—"

"An' the candied peel in the clove ones," Hallie added. "But maybe better have lunch now, Mis' Charlotta, before packin' all those."

By twilight the tree was trimmed and Lorrie sat on her stool, pleasantly tired from stretching, bending, walking around and around it to set some basket, ornament gingerbread piece, or cranberry string in just the proper place.

It did not look very much like the trees one could see in other windows up and down Ash Street. There were no lights, no sparkling ornaments, no trickling tinsel strips. But to Lorrie it was the most wonderful tree anyone could ever imagine. She said so.

"I think so, too, my dear. But it is out of another time and perhaps it has no place in the world outside these walls." Miss Ashemeade's hands lay quietly in her lap as she also looked at the tree. Sabina sat at the edge of her mistress' skirts, staring round-eyed at the strings of cranberry-popcorn, at some spinning ornaments that turned now and then, hanging beyond the reach of her claws.

Lorrie heard the chime of the mantle clock. Reluctantly she stood up. Then she looked from the tree to Miss Ashemeade.

"Thank you, oh, thank you!"

It was not only for the fun of trimming the tree, but also for this whole, long, beautiful day. Lorrie was not quite sure of her feelings, but she knew that she would remember all of this, and that memory would be something to treasure.

"Thank *you*, Lorrie. Yes—" again she seemed to read Lorrie's confused thoughts "—some memories are very good. They are a fire to warm one's heart. Do not forget, Lorrie, Christmas is coming."

"Christmas is coming," echoed Lorrie. Why had Miss Ashemeade said that? Of course, Christ-

mas was now only three days away, everyone
knew that. But the way Miss Ashemeade said
it, it sounded as if she were making a promise.

Lorrie said good night and struggled into her
ski pants, jacket, and boots in the hall. Hallie
had the mouse in a little bag and she let Lorrie
out into the bare garden where the unhappy
dragon pointed its snout at a dark sky.

As Lorrie came opposite the windows of the
room, she stopped for a last glimpse at the tree.
Several branches were in her range of vision. A
gingerbread lady leaned on one of them, her
rounded arm looped in a cranberry strand to
anchor her firmly on that perch, though she must
view with alarm the close-by swing of a white
sugar mouse.

Lorrie chuckled. The gingerbread lady had a
surprised look on her flat face. Hallie had given
her very arched eyebrows of frosting above her
eye currants. Perhaps she was just about to swing
away from the menacing mouse, using the chain
for transportation. What would Miss Ashemeade
or Hallie think if the lady gave a screech and
flew out into the room?

A cold wind reached Lorrie. She trotted on
along the brick walk. In the front yard the deer
had a ridge of snow on his back, some touches
of it in the curves of his antlers. But that did not
seem to bother him. He seemed as proud and
important as he always was. Lorrie waved her

hand to him and closed the gate carefully behind her. The Christmas tree lights were bright along the street. If she hurried she could arrange a surprise for Aunt Margaret, a live-looking sugar mouse under her supper napkin! Lorrie began to run.

Chole and Nackie

"OF COURSE, properly trimmed, there would be candles," Miss Ashemeade's voice made a calm whisper in the room. "But such candles would be difficult to find, and even more difficult to guard against fire. We used to keep a bucket of water standing on hand, just in case."

The firelight was warm, the many candles in holders about the red room were warm too, friendly with their light. Miss Ashemeade's table and frame were still against the wall, well out of the way. Now the room seemed centered about her and the tree.

Again she had changed her usual green dress for another. This was of garnet velvet. The wide skirt hung in soft folds over her knees, about the chair, to drape a little onto the floor. The lace collar was about her shoulders again, with cuffs to match at her wrists. She had no lace cap perched on her braids, but a high comb set in garnets winked there. And more of those red stones sparkled on her fingers and in the brooch pinning her collar. Nor was she wearing her black apron today. She looked, Lorrie thought, exactly as a fairy godmother should.

"But it is just perfect as it is!" Aunt Margaret sat on a footstool, aiming her camera at the tree. "I only hope that these pictures *do* turn out well. Those gingerbread figures and the ornaments— If I can *only* get a good shot!"

Lorrie nibbled at a piece of Hallie's candied peel, and blinked rather sleepily. She watched Sabina, a small black shadow, slip under the tree to where some parcels were laid, and reach a black paw for one.

"No!" Aunt Margaret cried and tried to wave the kitten away.

Sabina stared unblinkingly at Aunt Margaret for a moment, and then turned back to her own concerns. She took the package delicately between her teeth, brought it back to the hearth-rug where she began to remove its wrappings in long strips of shredded tissue paper. Miss Ashemeade laughed.

"That one knows her own mind. Well, perhaps she is right, it is time for the gifts. You know, one used to give presents on New Year's Day.

Christmas was for churchgoing and family gath-
erings. On New Year's one's friends came visiting
and then presents were exchanged. And, my how
cold some of those visitors might get on the
way! It was usually the gentlemen who came,
ladies stayed home to do the receiving. Afterward
young ladies counted their cards, to see who had
the most and the prettiest—all pictures and silk
fringe—"

Miss Ashemeade was looking at the tree, but
Lorrie thought she was really seeing things she
remembered.

"What kinds of presents were there?" Lorrie
asked after a pause.

"Presents? Oh, when one was very young a
jumping rope with wooden handles, or a porce-
lain slate. Dolls, to be sure, and a bangle
bracelet. Once, Lorrie, that workbox you use
now, all correctly fitted with scissors, silver thim-
ble, stiletto, needlecase, penknife, thread—Once
the music box. And always candy, maple cakes,
animals of barley sugar, gingerbread people—

"Then, when one grew older, there were other
things." But Miss Ashemeade did not list those.
Instead she reached out with her cane and neatly
snared one of the packages under the tree by
placing its tip through a ribbon bow. Balancing
it with ease, she held it out to Aunt Margaret.

"See what tricks infirmity can teach one? I
am proud of such sleight of hand." She slid the

package off her cane to land on Aunt Margaret's knees.

"Now, let us see if I can continue to do as well." She fished to catch a second bow, and with the same success transferred to Lorrie's hold another package.

Miss Ashemeade's gifts for them were wrapped in white tissue and tied with bright red ribbons. Lorrie laid hers carefully on the floor and went to take those she and her aunt had brought with them from under the tree. Two she handed to Miss Ashemeade, the other two she carried to Hallie sitting in one of the chairs beside the fireplace.

"Ah." Miss Ashemeade held up the one wrapped in the peacock-feather paper. "These new gift papers are works of art, are they not? Peacock feathers—those recall memories, do they not, Hallie?"

"Nackie's mats, Mis' Charlotta. It's easy remembrin' those. They was the sun 'n' moon 'n' stars to Nackie, an' maybe he was right."

Sabina growled. She had brought a catnip mouse out of what she plainly considered entirely unnecessary wrappings and was tossing it high in the air, to be pounced upon and shaken vigorously.

"Sabina! Sabina, remember in this room you are a lady!" But the kitten paid no attention to Miss Ashemeade's warning.

"Alas, who among humans has ever impressed his will upon a cat." Miss Ashemeade laughed again. "We must just ignore her bad manners."

Moments later Lorrie stared down at the contents of the package Miss Ashemeade had handed her. Miranda? No! Miranda's body, yes, with Miranda's dress upon it. But not Miranda's head. For Miranda, for all her age and her dearness to generations of small girls, had been just a doll, with staring blue eyes, rigid ripples of painted hair, a rather expressionless face.

Lorrie touched the cheek of this new Miranda. It was as smooth to feel as Miranda's china had been, but it was far more like her own skin in color. And the hair on the small head, braided and looped somewhat in the same style as Miranda's modeled and painted locks had been, was, or felt like, real hair. The expression was real. Now she looked like one of the doll-house people—a little like Phebe—as if she might suddenly come alive, shake free of Lorrie's hold, to move and speak for herself. Lorrie drew a long and rather shaky breath, then she looked to Miss Ashemeade.

"No, not Miranda," Miss Ashemeade said. "Miranda has had her life and she was very old and tired. I think she deserves her rest, do you not? This is someone else. I will let you decide just who—you will know, when the proper time comes."

"Why—" Aunt Margaret stared at the frame

she had unwrapped. "You can't mean to give this—it is too much of a treasure!"

"Treasures are born of cherishing," Miss Ashemeade spoke almost briskly, as if she wanted no thanks, did not even consider it polite for Aunt Margaret to offer them.

Aunt Margaret met her eyes for a long moment. "This shall continue to be cherished."

Miss Ashemeade smiled. "Did you believe I needed such assurance? Ah." She slipped off Lorrie's carefully tied ribbons, unfolded the peacock paper with small deliberate movements of her fingers. Then she lifted the handkerchief. The lace and the big A—they had been on in the shop. But the wreath about that A—did any crooked stitches show? Lorrie frowned anxiously. "Thank you, Lorrie." Miss Ashemeade tucked the handkerchief in her belt, frilled up its edges, and Lorrie was content.

Hallie admired her pot holder, with its marching line of little figures, each carrying a bowl, or a knife, or a fork, a spoon, a kettle. She drew her finger along under them.

"My, this heah's a whole army of cooks. Can't never say now I need me some help in the kitchen!"

It had been dark and dreary when they had come to Octagon House, but now the sun flashed through the pointed spears of icicles hanging over the windows. Aunt Margaret caught up her camera and turned it upon Miss Ashemeade.

"May I?" she asked.

There was again a smile on Miss Ashemeade's face. "If you wish to."

Sabina startled Lorrie by rubbing against her. Having so attracted the girl's attention, she made for the door to the hall and pawed at it, looking back at Lorrie, her wishes made very clear. Lorrie went to open it and Sabina flashed across the hall, to paw at the kitchen portal in turn. Once more Lorrie obeyed her urging.

But the kitchen did not content the kitten either. She was through that in a flash, and the door she now wanted to open was the one Lorrie had found locked during her back-in-time visit.

She followed Sabina on into a short hall from which spiraled the stairway hugging the big central chimney of the house. But Sabina called with a note of irritation in her "merrow" at another door.

Now they were in the green bedroom and Lorrie realized she had made the other half circuit of the house. The door of the doll-house room was Sabina's goal and Lorrie hurried to that.

There was no fireplace in the doll-house room, yet it did not seem cold in there, in spite of a huge icicle and several small ones half barring the one window. It was light, also, though there were no candles or lamps here and the sun shone on the other side of the house.

Lorrie looked about her. The other times she

had been here the horse and the house had claimed and held her attention. Now she was trying to see how like was this room to the one into which Lotta had brought Phineas and Phebe. There was no chair, but there were still shelves fastened to the walls. No books or jars, crocks, bottles were there now. No bunches of dried plants hung on strings. She looked at the floor. The house and its base took up a large portion of the room, the horse more. But she still could see the faint outlines of the painted design that had been so much clearer in the doll house.

A faint tinkling drew Lorrie's attention to the house. Once more Sabina pawed at a chain dangling from one of the drawers. Lorrie moved forward, as if Miss Ashemeade were telling her she must do this. She knelt and turned the key, and pulled open the drawer. It was not the one that held the Phineas and Phebe dolls, but the next. And Lorrie was not in the least surprised to find another pair of small figures.

One was taller than either Phineas or Phebe, the other much smaller. She lifted out the larger one. The skin of the face and hands was a creamy brown, and the hair, just showing a little under a ruffled cap such as Hallie wore, was black and curly. The dress was like Hallie's too, except for the color, for this was a pale yellow and scattered over it were white flowers hardly larger than the head of a pin. Like Hallie she wore an apron that reached almost to the hem of her full skirt.

137

The second, smaller doll was a boy, much younger than Phineas. He wore a red-and-white shirt of minute checks, and blue jeans, with a red handkerchief tied three-cornered about his throat. He had the same creamy-brown skin as the woman doll, and his head was covered with tight black curls.

Lorrie laid the woman doll on her knee and took up the boy. Again the fine stitching on the clothes amazed her. How could one sew so perfectly on such small things? There was a small creaking sound—-

Lorrie looked up. Perhaps Sabina was not responsible this time, but the side of the doll house swung slowly open. Once more Lorrie faced the kitchen, the green bedroom, and the small room of the painted floor, twin to the one in which she sat.

There were no preparations for pie making on the table now. Instead it seemed as if a dinner must be in progress, with a course waiting ready to be served. Dishes and platters were set on the big table and on a smaller one on the side. The top of the stove was covered with pots and pans.

Lorrie put the woman doll by the tall dresser with its burden of dishes, and tried to stand the boy by the stove. Only he would not, or could not, stand. At last she settled him on a small stool.

About her a whirling flurry of snowflakes drove between her and the house. Then the snow cleared and Lorrie found she was not on the back of a horse as she had thought she would be, but cuddled down in a sleigh. There was a white fur rug pulled up almost as far as her shoulders, and her head was snug in a fur-lined hood. She shared the seat of the sleigh with someone else, and Lorrie turned her head quickly to view her companion.

She, too, wore a fur-bordered hood. In the late afternoon that shone red, the ruff of fur about her face glowed white. Lotta drove the sleigh with practiced ease. It was a small sleigh in the form of a swan with a proudly curving neck and a high-held head. The horse speeding along before that curve of swan neck was white too, but his harness was as red as Lotta's hood, and tassels and silver bells bounced and rang as he trotted briskly along. There was a smell of pine from some boughs resting across their laps, a Christmas-y smell.

"Merry Christmas, Lorrie!" Lotta's voice was clear even above the ringing of the bells. She was not a little girl any longer, but a young lady. But she was still Lotta, and Lorrie smiled back.

"Merry Christmas!"

It was so exciting, this dash along the snowy road with the ringing of the bells, the smell of pine, and all the rest of it. But ahead Lorrie did not see the rise of the red-brick walls as she expected. If they were bound for the shelter of

Octagon House, they still had some distance to go.

" 'Deck the halls with boughs of holly,' " Lotta sang. "We have pine if not holly, Lorrie. Ah, this is a good day."

"Yes!"

The snow spattered up from the horse's flying hoofs. Some of it stuck against the arching wings of the swan that protected the riders. It was crispy cold, but all but the tip of Lorrie's nose was cheerfully warm. She wriggled her hands and discovered that under the sleigh robe they were not only mittened but also protected by a muff.

"Where are we going?" Lorrie dared to ask when Octagon House still did not come into view, though they rounded two curves and could now see a good stretch of open country through which the road was a pair of ruts deep cut in the snow.

Lotta shook the reins as if to urge the horse to a brisker pace. "I—" she had begun when there sounded a long mournful howl. Their horse neighed. Two dogs bounded toward them, and behind them rode men on horseback. Again the bells on the harness tinkled as Lotta pulled on the reins. The horse slowed to a walk and finally stopped.

Lorrie felt a chill she had not known earlier. There was something about those dogs, the the mounted men behind them— She did not know why she had that shiver of fear, but she heard Lotta say softly:

"It is their thoughts you feel, Lorrie, reaching as shadows across the snow, darkening, spoiling it. It is what they have done, and what they would do, that we see coming before them—a taste on the wind."

There was a puff of wind in their faces and Lorrie smelled what was a ghost of an old and evil odor. Lotta continued:

"What you smell is the seed of fear, Lorrie. Never forget that fear has a seed, and it is cruelty. There are hunters and hunted, those who run and those who pursue."

One of the hounds had almost reached the sleigh. It raised its head and bayed. Lotta whistled, only a note or two, high and shrill, and the hound whined and leaped away.

"Your servant, ma'am." Lorrie had been watching the hound so closely she had not seen the first rider gallop forward to Lotta's side of the sled. The man in the saddle leaned forward a little as if to see them both better.

He wore a broad-brimmed hat tied on his head with a scarf that went over the top of his hat and down over his ears, being then wound and tied about his throat. His thick coat had the collar well turned up, and he had heavy gloves on his hands.

"Your wish, sir?" Lotta had given him no greeting.

"Not to disturb so lovely a pair of ladies, ma'am." He had a mustache that curled up at the tips stiffly as if, Lorrie thought, he had used hair spray to set it so, and a little pointed beard that waggeld up and down before his checkered muffler as he spoke. "Have you passed anyone on the road?"

"And your reason for asking?" Lotta counter-questioned.

"Miss Ashemeade, ma'am." A second rider had come up to join the first. His face was round and reddened with the nip of hours in the cold. Some spikes of fair hairs stuck out raggedly from beneath his fur cap, which was old and had bare and shiny spots where the hair had fallen out.

"Constable Wilkins," Lotta acknowledged.

"We'se huntin' runways, ma'am. These here are lawmen from down 'cross the river. Two o' them runaways, ma'am, a woman an' a boy. It's the bounden duty of all law-bidin' folks to turn 'em in, ma'am."

It seemed to Lorrie that Mr. Wilkins was uneasy and grew uneasier still as Lotta continued to look at him calmly, just as she had once looked at Phineas when he had raised suspicious objections to her offer of help.

"We have been advised of that law several times, Constable Wilkins. A woman and a boy, you say. This is cruel weather through which to be hunted."

"By their own choice, ma'am," the other man broke in, "entirely by their own choice. You have not seen them, of course." But Lorrie thought that was not quite a question, it was almost as if he expected Lotta to say no, and refused to believe that she spoke the truth.

"We have seen no one. And now, the hour grows late, and the wind grows colder. If you will permit me, gentlemen." Lotta slapped the reins, and the white horse settled to his collar. Lorrie thought that the man wanted to say more, but the sleigh was already on its way again. When she looked inquiringly at Lotta, she saw that the happy look had vanished from the older girl's face.

"It seems that trouble does walk the world, even on this night, Lorrie. And we are summoned to take a hand. So—" She clicked her tongue and shook the reins again and the white horse quickened pace.

Lorrie looked back. She could still see the men as black dots and she heard the dogs yelping. The trees of a long finger of woods were reaching out for the sleigh. And as the sleigh came into their shadow, Lotta pulled in the horse to a walk.

"Watch for a tree that is storm-split, Lorrie," she said. "That is our trail marker."

Lorrie saw it to their right among others and called out. Then they turned off the road into a way where the snow lay soft and unbroken, but where there must be some sort of trail, for Lotta drove confidently forward.

"A short cut, Lorrie. I do not think they will backtrack to follow us, but if they do we shall have an excuse for taking this way. Now—" She began to sing. That tune—Lorrie thought she had heard the tune—but the words she did not understand. Only, after some moments she found herself humming the melody. Up scale and down went those notes as they drove out of the woods again, down a slope, and turned into another marked road. Now they turned right, taking a direction that led back the way they had come.

Still Lotta sang, sometimes so low her voice

rose hardly above a murmur, sometimes louder than the chime of the bells. Then, all at once, she stopped, and Lorrie thought she was listening, as if she expected some answer from the bushes and trees lining the road ahead.

Once, very far away, there was the bay of a hound. And then there was a faint smile about Lotta's lips for an instant. But still she watched the way before them intently. They pulled up a hill and paused on its crown for a moment while the horse snorted and blew clouds of white breath, bobbing his head up and down.

The road sloped again before them, crossed a bridge, and then—yes, to the left ahead Lorrie saw familiar red bricks. That was Octagon House. And when she sighted it, the small nipping fear that had been with her since they had met the horsemen vanished.

"Slowly, Bevis!" Lotta called.

As if he understood her, the horse neighed and nodded his head vigorously. They went down the far side of the hill at a much slower pace. And still Lotta looked as if she were listening, expecting to hear something besides the thud of hoofs on the packed snow.

"Bevis!" They had come close to the bridge when Lotta's voice rang out and the horse halted. Now Lotta flung aside the fur robe in the sleigh and climbed out. Though she did not summon Lorrie to join her, the girl pulled out of the tangle of cover to follow.

Lorrie's long skirts dragged in the snow as she tried to hold them up, moving far slower and more clumsily than Lotta, who was peering down into the shadows beneath the bridge, just as she had on that other night when Phineas and Phebe had taken refuge there.

Lorrie heard no crying this time. But there was something else. Just as she had sniffed that evil smell when the riders had met the sleigh, so now did she feel fear—not her fear but one that spread to her from the dark by the water. And she stopped, uneasy.

"They are well away—" Lotta's soft voice carried. "Their hounds are running straight now on the wrong scent. Come out while there is time."

There was no answer. It seemed to Lorrie that the fear wave came more strongly. Now it hit her so that she could not move. But Lotta held out her hands to the dark pool of shadow.

"You need not fear us. Come while there is time. I can promise you a safe hiding place. But how long we have, I do not know."

Again silence. Then Lorrie saw a flicker of movement in the shadows. Out of them crawled a bent-over figure, hands and knees in the snow. It dragged behind it what might have been a cloak or shawl on which lay a heap of rags.

"I'se got to believe." It was a cry of pain. "I'se purely got to believe that, mis'."

Lotta ran forward, her outstretched hands falling to the shoulders of the crawling figure.

"Lorrie!" she called, and Lorrie struggled through the drift to join her.

Together they brought to her feet a tall skeleton of a woman, who shivered with great shudders running all through her too thin body.

"Nackie! Nackie!" She tried to stoop again to the bundle on the shawl and nearly fell until Lotta steadied her.

"Come!" she urged. "We have so little time! Lorrie, bring the baby."

Baby? Lorrie looked down at the bundle, which had neither stirred nor cried. Baby? Not quite believing, she stooped awkwardly and picked up the heap of rags on the snow-wet shawl. She *did* hold a small body and there was a tiny movement against her shoulder as she struggled against the weight of her skirts back up to the sleigh.

Somehow they all crowded into the seat and Lotta snapped the reins. Bevis trotted on, across the bridge up the lane, turned past the horse block to come to the door of a stable. Someone ran through newly falling flakes of snow to meet them.

"Miss Lotta?"

"Take care, Phineas. We may have visitors later."

The boy nodded. "If they come, I'll have some answers for 'em. Do you need help?"

"Not now. You're better out here for a while."

Lorrie still carried that small light bundle as

she went up a shoveled path behind Lotta and the woman they had found to the back door. Light shone in the windows and, as she came into the back hallway, she heard the murmur of voices. They turned into the kitchen. From beside the stove a girl turned to face them. Her eyes widened as she saw the woman Lotta supported. Then she ran to open the other door into the hallway, asking no questions. They made a swift journey across the green bedroom, then were in the room with the shelves and the painted floor. Lotta lowered the woman into the chair. For a moment she was limp, and Lorrie was afraid she would slip to the floor. Then with a visible effort she straightened up and held out her arms.

"Nackie—give me my Nackie!" Her demand was fierce and she stared at Lorrie angrily. Lorrie hastened to lay the baby in her arms.

Only, as the woman pulled the tattered coverings from around that small body, Lorrie saw it was not a baby she had carried. It was an older child, with large eyes in a pinched face. He put up his hands and stroked the cheeks of the woman bending over him, and he made a sound, a rasping little cry that was no word or any normal child's call.

"Nackie!" The woman rocked back and forth in the chair, holding him close. Lotta went to the door. The girl from the kitchen—it was

Phebe—stood there holding a tray with a bowl and a mug on it.

Lotta brought them to the woman. "Drink. It is hot and nourishing and you need it."

The woman stared at her and took the mug, sipped from it, then held it to the child's lips. He drank greedily, and over his head she looked again to Lotta.

"We'se runaways, from 'cross th' river."

"I know. But here you are safe."

It was almost as if the woman could not understand. "Nackie—they was goin' t' sell me 'way from Nackie! They never did want him. He can't talk ner walk. He couldn't live weren't he with his ma. But he ain't trash like you throw 'way. He can do things with his hands. Looky here, mis', jus' looky here. Nackie made this all by his ownself!"

She took the cup away from the boy and put it on the tray Lotta still held, to search in the front of the shapeless garment she wore. Then she brought out a small square of woven mat. Its edging caught the light to glisten brilliantly. Feathers, Lorrie saw—peacock feathers.

"Nackie—he made me that—made it all by himself for his own ma who loves him! He ain't lackin' in th' head, no, he ain't! No matter what ol' mis' said. I ain't losin' my Nackie! I heard 'em tell as how they was goin' to sell Chole—that's me, miss'. An' so I jus' took Nackie an' I ran—I ran as far an' as fast as I could."

"There will be no more running," Lotta said. "Now drink this good soup in the bowl, Chole. You are safe here."

"Is I, mis'? Be there any safe place for me an' Nackie?"

"There is." The firmness in Lotta's voice was convincing. "Lorrie, will you take this to Phebe?" She held out the tray with the now empty mug and bowl.

Lorrie went back to the hall. There were no candles or lamps here—it was very dark. She was a little afraid of that dark, for it seemed to move about while she stood still. Then the dark was gone and she sat on the floor before the doll house once again.

Storm Clouds

"Aunt margaret." Lorrie held open on her lap one of the costume books her aunt kept for reference. "How old do you suppose Miss Ashemeade really is?"

Aunt Margaret glanced up from her sketching pad.

"I haven't the slightest idea, Lorrie. From things she says—" Aunt Margaret's voice trailed off, and she looked puzzled.

"Look here, see this dress? It's like those Miss Ashemeade wears. But the book says it was worn in 1865! And that's over a hundred years ago. Why should Miss Ashemeade wear a dress over a hundred years old?"

"Probably because she wants to, Chick. But

her dresses are not over a hundred years old,
they are just made over from the old patterns.
Miss Ashemeade does not go out, you know.
Perhaps she likes dresses of older periods and
sees no reason why she cannot suit herself and
wear them. They are very beautiful. And material such as those cannot be found nowadays."

"Then where does Miss Ashemeade find them?"
persisted Lorrie.

"Perhaps she has stored lengths of material to
use. It was often the custom to buy dress material by the bolt and store it for future use. In a
house as old as hers, there must be a good
supply of things from the past. Octagon House
was built back in the mid-1840's."

"Who built it?"

"The Ashemeade family. Miss Ashemeade is
the last of them now, at least the last of that
name in Ashton."

"Hallie wears dresses like these, too." Lorrie
went back to her first line of questioning.

"Hallie greatly admires Miss Ashemeade, and
she must be as old, so she likes the same styles.
I must admit, on both of them those dresses are
very becoming."

Lorrie turned back the pages of the book and
looked at another illustration and at the date
beneath it. Miss Ashemeade wore a dress of 1865,
but the little girl in this other illustration had a
dress like that of the doll Phebe. And the date
under it was 1845.

She began to turn the pages carefully in search of something else. The full skirts were common and she could see no small detail to date the dress Lotta had worn during that journey by sleigh. And—who was Lotta?

Once or twice Lorrie had believed she knew. Only that could not be true! Or—could it? She turned back to the page of Miss Ashemeade's dress.

"What a wonderful house!" Aunt Margaret was no longer working, but looking rather at the wall where hung her Christmas gift from Miss Ashemeade. It was a picture of a lady and gentleman standing stiffly in a garden where flowers grew stiffly also. The gentleman had long curls that hung down on his shoulders, and a sword at his side. Aunt Margaret explained that it was stump work, a kind of embroidery very seldom seen, and that the picture must be close to three hundred or more years old. "It is really a museum, Lorrie."

"Then, why doesn't someone make it one? They couldn't tear it down for the thruway if it were a museum, could they?" demanded Lorrie.

"Perhaps." Aunt Margaret picked up her sketching pencil again as if she did not want to talk about that. "Don't you have some home-work, Chick?"

Lorrie put the costume book back in its proper place. "Math," she said briefly and with no relish. But it was hard to think of math when this other idea had taken root in her mind.

If Octagon House was made important they could not pull it down. How did you make a house important? A story in the paper—maybe talking about it on TV? But how did one get a story in the paper, or someone to talk on TV? Did you just write a letter and ask?

"Lorrie, you don't seem to have done very much," Aunt Margaret observed as she gathered her own papers together and slid them into her brief case. "I don't believe Mrs. Raymond will accept such scribbling. If I remember rightly from my own school days, once Christmas was over it was back to work, and hard work, before the end of the term."

"Yes, I guess so." Lorrie tried to push Octagon House out of her mind and concentrate on the dreary figures that she never liked.

But in bed that night she thought again about Octagon House. Suppose she, Lorrie Mallard, could write a letter to the newspaper, all about the house and Miss Ashemeade, and the wonderful things—

Wonderful things— Lorrie's enthusiasm about her budding idea was sharply checked. The doll house—Miss Ashemeade had never mentioned the house to Lorrie, just as she herself had never spoken of it to Miss Ashemeade, or to Aunt Margaret. It was—it was something very private, Lorrie knew without anyone telling her so. But it was part of Octagon House and if that were turned into a museum— Miss Ashemeade and Hallie—where would they live? Did people ever live in museums? But what if—if the house were torn down—then where would Miss Ashemeade and Hallie go? And where would the doll house and Bevis and—and Sabina—go? Lorrie sat up in bed. What *would* happen? She had to tell—to ask Miss Ashemeade. Tomorrow she would get away from school as fast as she could and—

Oh—tomorrow they had the class meeting. But that did not matter, not now. She simply had to see Miss Ashemeade and ask her about the museum idea, about whether it could be done.

Lorrie was impatient. All her life she had always wanted to do at once anything she had planned. But now she must wait through the night, and most of tomorrow, before she could see Miss Ashemeade. She twisted uneasily on her pillow as she lay down again.

She dreamed that she saw the house and over it a big storm cloud. In the shadow of that the red-brick walls began to shrink smaller and smaller until Lorrie was afraid that they would vanish altogether. She ran forward, trying to reach the house before it disappeared. But suddenly the front door opened, and Miss Ashemeade stood there. She was not leaning on Hallie's arm, nor was she depending on her cane for support, but she held out both hands, waving

Lorrie back. And she was smiling as if all were well.

However in the morning her plan still filled Lorrie's mind. Kathy pounded on the door and they went off together, taking the shorter way that did not go down Ash Street. Kathy chattered busily as usual but suddenly she broke off and said in a sharper voice:

"Lorrie Mallard, I don't think you've heard one single, solitary word I've said. Where are you anyway? Right here, or about a billion miles away?"

Lorrie was startled out of her own thoughts. "Here—at least I'm walking along this street."

"You'd never know it to look at you! You're more like one of those robots Rob keeps reading about. I was talking about Valentine Fair and Open House, Lorrie—THE VALENTINE FAIR!"

"But Valentine Day's in February, and this is only January."

"Boy, are you ever a real drippy dope, Lorrie. The Valentine Fair is about the biggest thing at school, it surely is. We're the seniors this year, and that means we plan most of it. And today they are going to elect both committees—girls' and boys'."

"You ought to be on it, Kathy."

"I sure hope so. Look here, Lorrie. Deb Collins said she'd nominate me. Now, will you second it?"

"You mean get up in class and say I want you for the committee?"

"You just say, 'Second the nomination.' Lorrie, you've heard them do it before, there's nothing to it. I've some dreamy ideas and I think I have a chance to be chairman. So, you'll do it, won't you?"

"But—I wasn't going to stay for the meeting."

Kathy stared at her. "Whyever not? And, don't be stupid, Mrs. Raymond won't let you miss it, anyway. Being seniors we're supposed to take an intelligent interest. Don't you remember what she said last week? Or weren't you listening then either?"

"I have something important to do," protested Lorrie.

"I'm telling you the truth, it's got to be the best excuse in the world or Mrs. Raymond isn't going to take it. You'll be there, Lorrie. Now, will you second me for the committee?"

"Yes." Lorrie's heart sank. Kathy was probably right, she so often was in such matters. And if she had to stay for the class meeting, she would have no time for a visit to Octagon House tonight. But it was so important!

Kathy was right. Lorrie tried her excuse of an important errand after school. But when the questioning revealed to Mrs. Raymond that the errand was Lorrie's idea and not Aunt Margaret's, she was told that participation in class activities was far more important.

Lorrie returned to her seat with a rush of the same unhappy feeling that had been hers when she had first come to Ashton. She was hardly aware of Bill Crowder's calling the class to order as president and the rest of the talk at the front of the room. But she came to with a start when she was conscious of a sudden silence. Several of those around her were glancing at Lorrie as if they expected something from her, and she had a sudden thrust of panic—as if she had been called upon to recite and had not heard the question.

Then two seats beyond, Bessie Calder stood up and said, "I second the nomination."

I second the nomination! Why, that was what Kathy had asked her to say! Kathy! Lorrie glanced quickly at Kathy and met an accusing stare in return. Kathy had asked her, and she hadn't done it. Kathy must believe she kept quiet on purpose!

Again Lorrie ceased to listen to what was going on as she thought furiously of how she could explain her lapse to Kathy. She would have to tell Kathy about Octagon House and the thruway. Now she shifted impatiently in her seat, waiting for the end of the meeting so she could get to Kathy and explain.

Only Lorrie was not to have the chance, because, as she started toward Kathy's desk, the other girl called:

"Bess! Chris! Wait up! I've some groovy ideas. Just wait until you hear them!"

Lorrie pushed her way determinedly to Kathy's desk. "Kathy—Kathy!" she called, intent on making Kathy turn her head and acknowledge her being there. She made some impression, for Kathy did turn and look around. But her face was set and cold.

"What do you want, Lorrie Mallard? You broke your word. Think I want you on *my* committee now?"

"But Kathy—"

"I said"—Kathy leaned over her desk—"get lost, Lorrie. You wouldn't help me, I don't need you—and don't you forget it! Come on, gang, we've got a lot to do!"

With that she joined a waiting group of girls and was gone. Lorrie pulled her book bag back to her locker. There was no hurry now, she did not have time enough to go by Octagon House, and she was not about to leave so fast Kathy would believe she was trailing along behind her. As Kathy had pointed out, they did not need each other—not at all. Lorrie kept holding to that thought as she zipped up her ski jacket. Someone banged the door of the locker next to hers and she looked up.

"Lizabeth—"

"Out in the cold again, Lorrie?" Lizabeth asked. "What did you do this time to upset her

159

royal highness?" There was such sharpness in Lizabeth's voice that Lorrie was startled.

"She asked me to second her nomination for the committee and—well, I was thinking about something else and I forgot all about it. She has a right to be mad."

"Now"—Lizabeth set her hands on her hips and looked at Lorrie—"now just what could be more important than this committee? What deep thought, Lorrie?"

Lorrie felt a little embarrassed. Lizabeth did not like Kathy, not one little bit. And she made it so clear now. Lorrie thought back to the theater party and her own uneasiness about how Kathy had acted over the seating. Lizabeth had so quickly withdrawn then into a shell of her own.

"I was worried." Suddenly she had to talk to someone and she liked Lizabeth, or the usual Lizabeth, not this sharp-tongued one. "Lizabeth, do you know the Octagon House?"

"That old place over on Ash Street? Sure. Daddy says it's the only one of its kind anywhere around—has eight sides. What about it?"

"They say it's going to be torn down for the thruway."

"Yes, the line runs through from Gamblier Avenue to the State route, and that's three blocks beyond Ash."

"How do you know so much?"

"Daddy's on that project, he's an engineer

with the highways. But what about you, why do you care where the thruway goes?"

"They can't tear down Octagon House!" Lorrie protested. "I thought— Suppose people wrote to the papers and said not to— Or someone talked on the TV about it. Wouldn't that stop them?"

"They've been doing that for over a year now," Lizabeth returned. "Oh, not writing about Octagon House, but about other houses. This Friday they're having a big meeting about it before the Commissioners. But it isn't going to do them any good. There's a river underground a little to the north, and they can't build the thruway over that, so it will have to go this way."

"A river?" Lorrie repeated. Was it perhaps the stream that the bridge had spanned in the past, under which the fugitives had hidden?

"Yes. It used to be above ground, just like any other. Then they began to build more and more houses out here. So finally they put the river in big pipes and built right over it. But they can't lay the thruway over that."

"But Octagon House—"

"And what makes that so wonderful? They're going to tear down the old Ruxton House too. And Mother says that's a shame. A man came all the way from England more'n a hundred years ago to plan that. It's beautiful."

"So is Octagon House," countered Lorrie stubbornly.

161

"Now? It's an old wreck on a piece of wild land."

Lorrie shook her head. "It only looks wild from outside the fence, Lizabeth. Inside there's a garden, and in the house— Oh, Lizabeth, it's wonderful!"

"How do you know? Lorrie Mallard, have you been *in* the witch house, have you really?"

"There's no witch!" Lorrie flared. "There are Miss Ashemeade and Hallie and Sabina! And my aunt says it's like a museum there. Yes, I've been in, and so has Aunt Margaret. I go there to learn sewing from Miss Ashemeade, and Aunt Margaret's been there to Sunday tea, and we were there on Christmas. It was wonderful! You ought to have seen the tree and Hallie's gingerbread people and—" Lorrie launched into a confused description of Octagon House, its inhabitants and treasures—all but the horse Bevis and the doll house. And Lizabeth listened with flattering interest.

"You girls there—time to get out." It was Mr. Haskins, the janitor, shouting at them down the hall. Lorrie slammed shut her locker.

Why, it must be late. Everyone else had gone. She looked up to the big clock at the end of the hall just as its minute hand made a full sweep —ten after four!

"Look here," Lizabeth said, "Mother's calling for me. I'm supposed to go to the dentist. We can let you off at the end of Ash and you don't have far to go from there, do you?"

"Mother," Lizabeth announced as they reached the waiting car, "we can drop Lorrie off at the corner of Ash, can't we? It's late."

"As I was just about to observe. What kept you, Lizabeth? Of course, Lorrie, hop in."

Lizabeth wriggled into the middle of the front seat. "Mother, Lorrie's been in the Octagon House, she knows Miss Ashemeade. And they had a Christmas tree with gingerbread people."

"So you know Miss Ashemeade, Lorrie?" Mrs. Ross's voice cut through her daughter's excited speech. "That is a privilege, Lorrie."

"Do you know her, too, Mrs. Ross?"

"When I was a little girl, I went there twice with my aunt. Her father's aunt lived there— Hallie Standish."

"Hallie's still there!" said Lorrie eagerly. "She made the gingerbread people for the tree and all the little candies."

"But—" Mrs. Ross looked startled. "But she can't be! Why, Auntie would be in her late eighties if she were still living. And Hallie—why Hallie Standish would have to be over a hundred! It must be her daughter. Though," Mrs. Ross looked thoughtful, "I didn't know she had a daughter. But I do remember my visits there and Miss Ashemeade—she must be very old now."

"Mrs. Ross, what will happen to Miss Ashemeade and Hallie if they tear down Octagon

House? And can't they save the house? Aunt Margaret says it is like a museum."

"Nothing is decided, it won't be until after the Commissioners' meeting. Most of the people will be represented by lawyers. Surely Miss Ashemeade will. Oh, here's your corner, Lorrie."

"Thank you, Mrs. Ross." Lorrie watched the car draw away and then she started down Ash Street. When she reached the fence about Octagon House she slowed. She could see the deer, who had snow piled high about the base on which he stood but none now on his back, and the shuttered front windows, the closed door. She put her hand to the gate, and tried to work the catch. But it did not give under her fingers and somehow she knew this was not the time to climb into territory closed against her. Unhappily Lorrie went on toward the apartment house a block away.

Kathy—she must explain to Kathy, Lorrie thought as she went down the hall, though she was uncomfortable as she pressed the button of the Lockner doorbell. Rob answered.

"Kathy? No, she's over at Bess Calder's for supper. She's really flipped over this Valentine Fair. Valentines!" he laughed. "They're for girls."

"Tell her I want to see her," Lorrie said. She was sure, though, that if she did see Kathy it would be by her own efforts, with no help from Kathy.

And her fears proved true. The next morning

she lingered, waiting for Kathy, not quite daring to go to the Lockner apartment again. But no Kathy appeared and Lorrie was almost tardy, making her desk only a second or two before Mrs. Raymond closed the door. Kathy was in her place but Lorrie had no time to speak to her.

Recess was just as bad. When the bell rang, Kathy asked permission to hold a committee meeting in the room and Lorrie had to go out with the others, leaving Kathy and her friends in a group about Mrs. Raymond's desk. Toward the end of the day, as Kathy continued to avoid every attempt Lorrie made, Lorrie lost her temper. So, let her think what she wanted to! She, Lorrie, was through trying to explain! She had more important things to think about and today she was going to stop at Octagon House. If the gate was shut, why she would just climb over it! But she had to see Miss Ashemeade—she had to.

However the gate did swing open slowly and gratingly under her push. Lorrie was breathing fast, as she had run most of the way from school in order to have time for this visit. But surely Aunt Margaret would understand if she were a little late getting home. Aunt Margaret was concerned too. The meeting with the Commissioners was this week, and Miss Ashemeade must have some way to make them understand the importance of Octagon House.

Lorrie ran around the house and knocked on the back door. For the first time Hallie did not answer. A little frightened, Lorrie tried the latch and it lifted. She came slowly into the hall.

"Hallie?" she called.

The door to the kitchen was shut, but the one to Miss Ashemeade's room a little ajar.

"We are in here, Lorrie."

Lorrie tugged at zippers, pulled off at top speed the ski suit to hang pants and coat on the wall pegs and set her boots under. Then she went in, only to stop just inside the door and look ahead with startled eyes. Hallie was working by the long table. She was flanked by tall cartons with detergent advertisements stamped on their sides (they looked as out of place in this room as a pile of dirty boards).

Sabina stood on her hind legs scraping her front claws down the side of one box, trying vainly to see into its interior. Into the next one Hallie was carefully packing all the rolls of materials and ribbon that had lain undisturbed on that end of the table ever since Lorrie had first come here. There was the rustle of tissue paper as she rolled each one in that covering before fitting it into the carton.

Packing—Hallie was packing things away! Was—had Miss Ashemeade given up? Was she planning to move? But there was nowhere else for Miss Ashemeade, and Hallie, and all the treasures of Octagon House. This was where they had belonged. They could not live anywhere else and be the same!

"Housecleaning, Lorrie." Miss Ashemeade was busy, too. The length of tapestry that had been in the frame, for which Lorri had threaded so many needles of wool, lay across her lap, and she was folding it carefully in a piece of protecting muslin. "Things accumulate so, and every once in a while they must be put to rights. It is an offense against thrift to hold onto what one cannot use to any profit. Hallie's box is going to the Ladies Aid of the Gordon Street Church. They can put all those pieces to good use, better use than they will be here, attracting dust and getting creased and faded. Why, what is the matter, my dear?"

"You're—you're not packing to move? You're not leaving Octagon House—"

Miss Ashemeade raised her hands and held them out, and Lorrie was drawn to her as if those hands had reached clear across the long room to her. When she stood beside Miss Ashemeade's chair, they came to rest on her shoulders.

"You need never fear, Lorrie, about that. I shall not leave Octagon House, nor shall the house—the real house—ever leave me."

"The real house—"

But Miss Ashemeade was shaking her head. "The time will come, Lorrie, when you shall understand that. So, you thought we were moving, not cleaning up a bit? Ah, Lorrie, were we to move, I am afraid we would have to pull up roots so long and deep set that there would be

167

a major disturbance in the world. Is that not so, Hallie?"

" 'Deed so, Mis' Charlotta, 'deed so." Hallie chuckled. "Cleanin' up, that ain't movin', Mis' Lorrie. Now, looky heah, Sabina, you take's your claws outa that right smart. Them fixings was never meant for pullin' about thataway."

Sabina was backing across the carpet, pulling after her a long trail of golden ribbon that uncoiled as she went. She tried to jerk it free from Hallie's fingers when Hallie caught the other end. But Hallie won that tug of war and rewound the ribbon, to put it in the carton.

"Housecleaning is an excellent occupation for

at least once a year," Miss Ashemeade continued. "And not only houses need cleaning. But, Lorrie, you are still troubled. Now tell me what it is."

"Tomorrow night is the meeting with the Commissioners, Miss Ashemeade, about the thruway."

"And you are wondering if I shall be represented there. Yes, there is a Mr. Thruston who will see to my interests."

"I've been thinking, if people wrote letters to the papers, maybe talked on the TV and the radio—Aunt Margaret said this house was a museum. Museums are important, they can't go knocking those down. Maybe Octagon House might be a museum if people wanted it."

Miss Ashemeade smiled slowly. "A museum, yes, that is what it has become through the years, Lorrie, but not one that everyone can enjoy. Museums have no real life, they are full of things frozen in time, so stand always as they are. There are those who enjoy visiting them to see the past, but those who feel true kinship with the past grow fewer and fewer."

She looked about the room. "There are treasures here, Lorrie, as your aunt saw, which perhaps do belong in a place where they may be cared for and shown to those who appreciate them for their history and their beauty. But this house holds other treasures that cannot be reckoned by the measurements of the world outside its walls. No, good as your plan is in its way, my dear, it cannot be used to protect Octagon House. Now"—again she looked at Lorrie—"do not carry this worry as a burden, my dear. There is a solution, believe me there is. You have nothing to fear for Octagon House, nothing at all."

And Lorrie believed. She gave a sigh of relief. Mr. Thruston must be an extra-special lawyer.

"Now, Lorrie, how goes the world with you? You may put these wools to rights while you tell me."

Lorrie sat down on her old place on the stool and began to untangle and rewind the odds and ends of wools left from the tapestry, tucking the loose ends under neatly. She found herself talking about Kathy and the trouble her own absent-mindedness had caused.

"Valentines," Miss Ashemeade said. "A Valentine Fair to raise money for the school. Lorrie, see that large scrapbook over there, on the bottom shelf of the case? Bring it here, child."

Lorrie brought over the large book. It was bound in leather of dark red, embossed and stamped with a design that combined small, plump hearts and wreaths of flowers. And in the creases of the design there were still faint lines of gold.

"Take it with you, Lorrie. And tonight tell Kathy you have something very special to show her. Tell her also, that if she is interested, to do what comes into her mind and that you will help her."

"What—?" Lorrie started to open the book, but Miss Ashemeade shook her head.

"No. Open it with Kathy, my dear. And remember—tell her you can help her. That is all. Now, perhaps you had better go, it is getting late. Let Sabina out for her run as you leave. Do not worry about us, Lorrie. We are going to manage splendidly."

She was so certain that she made Lorrie certain of that, too.

Charles

THE BOOK was big, too big to put into Lorrie's bag, and she had been afraid she would drop it in the snow, so she gave a sigh of relief when she reached the apartment lobby.

"Then I'll see about the cookies—"

Lorrie halted just inside the door. Kathy and Bess were there. They both turned around to look at her as she came in.

"Hello, Lorrie," Bess said, as if she did not know just what to say and chose the easiest words.

"Hello." Lorrie marched straight for Kathy. Maybe Kathy would turn and go upstairs, with Bess seeing and listening to everything. But this was the best chance she had had since the unfortunate class meeting to talk to Kathy. "This time, Kathy, you have to listen."

"I don't have to," Kathy interrupted. But Lorrie stood right in front of her now, and her refusal trailed into silence.

"I wasn't trying to be mean, Kathy, when I didn't second your nomination at the meeting. I was thinking about something else, something important, and I really forgot what was going on."

"Forgot!" Kathy looked unconvinced. "As if you *could*—"

"I did, and that's the truth, Kathy Lockner, the whole truth!"

"I don't see what could be so important that you'd forget like that." Kathy's protest sounded less certain.

"It was important to me, Kathy. Now"—she held out the book—"I have something for you to see. Miss Ashemeade said you should."

"Who's Miss Ashemeade?" Kathy demanded, but she was looking at the scrapbook.

"The lady who lives in Octagon House."

"She means the old witch!" broke in Bess.

Lorrie spun around. "You take that back, Bess Calder—right now you take that back! Miss Ashemeade's nice. She had Aunt Margaret and me there for Christmas, and it was wonderful. And Octagon House is beautiful."

"It's an old eyesore, my father says so," shrilled Bess. "And the city's going to tear it down and put a street right over it, so there, Lorrie Mallard! You'd better take your old witch's book and get out. Kathy and me's talking committee business and you're not on the committee. Kathy wouldn't have you after what you did!"

But Kathy was still looking at the book Lorrie held. "What is it?" she wanted to know.

"A scrapbook. I haven't looked in it either. Miss Ashemeade said to wait for you. Come on up"—she hesitated and then added to Bess—"both of you and let's see."

"All right," Kathy agreed. "You, too, Bess. Call your mother and stay for supper if she lets you. It's almost five anyway."

"But what right's Lorrie got pushing in? She isn't on the committee."

"Who said anything about this being for the fair? Miss Ashemeade said to show it to Kathy."

"How did she know about me?"

"I told her about what happened and how sorry I was that I forgot. And I am sorry, Kathy, but you wouldn't let me say so before."

"All right. Come on, Bess, let's see—won't hurt us."

Lorrie unlocked the door and went to lay the book on the coffee table. A moment later she turned the thick leather cover to the first page.

"Valentines!" Bess exclaimed.

Valentines they were, fastened to each page, but such valentines!

"See this round one!" Kathy touched with a finger tip. "Those flowers, they're really embroidered in silk! And look at the darling little cupid holding up the wreath of roses!"

"And that one. It must be a paper doll, isn't it, Lorrie?" Bess added her voice to Kathy's. "But the dress—it's so old-fashioned!"

"Look at this one! The center is satin and the lady's painted on—with the butterflies." Kathy had found another wonder. "Why, Lorrie, I never knew they once had valentines like these—all lace and flowers, with birds and butterflies."

"They're a lot prettier than the kind we have now. Oh, here's one that's an open fan with a lot of pictures at the top and a cord and tassel at the bottom!"

"They're old," Lorrie said thoughtfully. "But that lace, it's rather like the lace you see now in paper mats. Aunt Margaret has some for cake plates."

"These flowers and birds." Bess touched one bluebird. "Don't they have little books at the bookshop—the gummed-stamp ones? Some are flowers and some are birds. You know, the first graders get them pasted on good papers at school."

"This one has real lace on it." Kathy bent closer. "I've seen edging at the fabric shop that looks like these tiny pink roses."

"Did you see Lizabeth's Christmas cards? Wait a minute, let me show you." Lorrie put down the book and went to get a card from the desk drawer. "She made them herself. I asked her where she got the pictures for them, and these gold stars and leaves, and she told me about a store that has all kinds of these. They come from Germany. Now, doesn't this little angel look a lot like the cupid on that card?"

Kathy took the Christmas card to make a careful comparison.

"It does," she admitted, but Lorrie thought she did so reluctantly.

"Lizabeth could show us the store."

"You and Lizabeth are not on the committee!" Bess set back on the couch. "Kathy?" She looked to her in appeal.

Kathy was still studying the pages before her. "See here, Bess, we want to make money for the senior gift, don't we? Well, we have a cooky table, just as always, and a candy table. But this kind of thing, we've never tried before. And I'll bet it would be something even the grownups would like. You know, Mother and I went to visit a friend of hers, a Mrs. Lacy who lives up on Lakeland Heights. And she had a coffee table with a glass top. Under that were some valentines like these."

"But those were real old ones, like those in this book," Bess pointed out, "not like those made today."

"But they were pretty, so people saved them. Listen, Bess, how many valentines from last year did you have more'n a few weeks?"

Bess thought. "A couple."

"Because someone special sent them to you, not because they were so pretty. Now isn't that so?"

"I guess so."

"All right. But you offer some copies of these old ones for sale and perhaps people would keep them longer."

"We can't use these."

"No, I said copies." Kathy studied Lizabeth's card again. "Lorrie, you say Lizabeth knows a store that sells these cutouts. Could you ask her where it is?"

"You ask her, Kathy," Lorrie answered calmly. "Lizabeth made that card, so she must know a lot about such work." She thought Kathy looked flushed and a little ill at ease. Then the committee chairman lifted her head with a little toss.

"All right, I will! As of now, Bess, we are

going to expand the committee. Lorrie comes in and Lizabeth, if they will."

"The rest of the girls aren't going to like it," Bess protested.

"Why not? We want to have the best Valentine Fair ever, don't we? And here's something no other class ever had before. The boys are going to put on a puppet show and run the pop booth, and Jimmy Purvis will show his animal slides. But they've always had something like that—as they always had the candy and cooky sales. Now, this is something new and I think it's good!"

"But asking Lizabeth—"

Kathy turned sharply. "All right, Bess, just go on and say it! Say you don't want to be on a committee with her."

"You said it, too, and other things—" Bess stopped short under Lorrie's accusing stare. Kathy was very flushed.

"Yes," Kathy admitted in a low voice, "I did."

"And now—just because you think she can do something for your old committee, you're ready to ask her!" Bess returned.

Lorrie looked from Bess to Kathy, who was very red now. Maybe that was the truth. But she remembered what Aunt Margaret had said— walls rose because people did not really know each other. If they did get to know, the walls began to crumble.

"Lizabeth's nice," she said, "and she's clever. She's one of the smartest girls in the class and you both know it. She should be on the committee anyway and, I think if Kathy asks her in the right way, she will."

"And what's the 'right way'?" Bess wanted to know.

"Tell her that she has something the class needs," Lorrie said slowly. "That's really what a committee is, isn't it. People all working together, each doing what he can, even if they don't all do the same things?"

Kathy nodded. "All right, I'm going to ask her. Maybe it's because she can work. But some people don't care for Sandra Tottrell very much, and we asked her because she makes super fudge. Isn't that so, Bess?"

Bess was frowning. "It's your committee." She sounded grudging.

"It's our fair," Kathy returned. "Lorrie, would Miss Ashemeade let us borrow this book for a while, so we could copy ideas from it? We would promise you could take charge of it and we would be very careful."

"I'll ask."

"You might go through it tonight," Kathy continued, "and make a list of things we need, lace paper and flower seals and ribbon. Then maybe Saturday we could see about buying them. And tomorrow at recess, if you could bring the book, Lorrie, we'll show the girls and decide."

"I'll see if Miss Ashemeade will let me."

"Come on, Bess, you have supper with us, and

then we'll do some phoning to the committee. Thanks, Lorrie, and thank Miss Ashemeade too."

But when Aunt Margaret came home and Lorrie showed her the scrapbook and explained, Aunt Margaret shook her head.

"Lorrie, these old valentines are what they term 'collectors' items' now and are undoubtedly worth a great deal of money. I don't like your bringing them here, and certainly you should not take them to school tomorrow."

"But Miss Ashemeade gave me the book, told me to show Kathy—"

"To show Kathy in our home, not to carry it to school where an accident might happen. No, Lorrie. And I do not think we should keep it here. As it happens I have some of the Christmas pictures back from the developer and I want to give Miss Ashemeade a set. So, after supper, we shall return the book. It is far too precious to be handled carelessly. Miss Ashemeade may not realize its value."

Hurriedly Lorrie leafed through the pages and tried to list the supplies Kathy wanted. But could they do anything without the samples in the book to copy? Maybe she had made Kathy believe something that now could not be carried out.

The front of Octagon House was very dark when she and Aunt Margaret arrived before the gate. But the latch gave under Lorrie's push and, as they took the walk around the house, they saw the gleam of lamp and candlelight in the windows of the red room. Also it seemed that they might have been expected, for Hallie opened the back door at their first knock.

"Come in, come in. This is a chill night!" She welcomed them heartily. "Go right in with you now. An' git close to the fire, toast your fingers and toes!"

Aunt Margaret knocked on Miss Ashemeade's door and, at her low call went in, the scrapbook in her hand. She had carried it from the apartment in a plastic bag, as if she feared something would happen to it. But when Lorrie would have followed her, Hallie set her old wrinkled hand on her shoulder and gave her a little push toward the kitchen instead.

Surprised, Lorrie went. This room was warm and welcoming also. Sabina sat upright in the chair by the stove. Hallie moved to the table and lifted a hot cooky from a sheet on the tip of a turner.

"Seems like I was jus' knowin' someone would be along tonight. Now you wraps your tongue about this, child, an' then you lets me know how it does taste."

Lorrie obediently tasted, until the cooky was all gone. "Mmmmmm, extra, special good! That's what it is, Hallie!"

"You ain't th' furst as has said that, Mis' Lorrie. You, Sabina, what is you up to now?"

Sabina had jumped from her chair and was

crying by the other kitchen door, the one that led to the hallway.

"Let her out, child. She has her own night ways, an' they ain't ours."

Lorrie opened the door. But somehow she already knew what Sabina wanted. The doll-house room—Sabina was leading her to the doll-house room. Licking the last crumbs from her fingers, Lorrie followed.

Moonlight fell very bright and clear on the house, made Bevis' hide coat silvery. Lorrie moved around the doll house. Oddly enough she could see illumination in the rooms. There were faint glows from the small lamps and candles, though she could not see any flames. And she was so intent upon peeking in an upper window that she struck her shin against an unnoticed, half-open drawer in the base.

This was a smaller drawer, set just under the room with the painted floor. Unlike the other two she had opened, this one held a single doll. Lorrie lifted it out and held it into the moonlight.

It was a man doll and it wore a uniform with a small sword at the belt. Lorrie saw a gray jacket with an upstanding tight collar, and scrolls of very fine gold on the sleeves. A Confederate soldier! He had a thin face with prominent cheekbones and rather long dark hair, and his eyes seemed alive, as if he were looking intently back at her.

Lorrie tried the back section of the house,

supposing it would swing open as it always had before. But this time it was firmly set. She walked around to try the other side. That gave, pulling out to show the parlor, the front hall, and the dining room, which was now Miss Ashemeade's day room.

In the parlor no cloths covered the furniture, the fire was built up in the grate. Carefully Lorrie set the soldier beside the fireplace, and knew that was where he belonged. She swung the side of the house back into place and went to Bevis. But this time she did not climb into the saddle, because that curious whirlabout came before she had time to. She heard Bevis' snort by her ear and turned her head. She had been in a moonlit room and she was still in moonlight. But this was outside and the moon was bright on snow. Bevis stamped and snorted again.

They were by the stable and there was a lantern there, hung over the main door.

"Miss Lotta, they're out beatin' th' river banks. You ain't goin' down there!" The voice in the stable was raised in hot protest.

"Not by the river, no, Phineas. I am going to the village."

"But you'll have to pass them, Miss Lotta. An' they're a rough lot. Let me go, I can take a note t' the rector."

"Phineas, what if I hadn't gone on a night we remember, or on another night Chole tries hard to forget?"

"But, Miss Lotta, this here's a Reb, outa prison. He's desperate and dangerous. They say as how he kilt a man as tried to stop him."

"They say, they say! Always *they* say many things, Phineas. No one has managed however, I notice, to mention the name of the man who was killed or even repeat the same story twice. At least not in my hearing. No, I'll ride to the village, Phineas, and what happens thereafter is a matter of fate and fortune. Do not fear for me, Phineas, never for me."

There was a muttering and then the door swung open. A white horse, twin to Bevis, came through, on his back a woman riding sidesaddle. She did not seem in the least surprised to find Lorrie in the lane, but smiled in greeting.

"A chill night, but light enough, Lorrie," she said. "Shall we ride?" She brought her mount close to Lorrie and reached down to aid her into the saddle. But Lotta did not speak again as they trotted to that other road, which wound much as Ash Street would run some day.

In the direction of the river, Lorrie saw bobbing lights and once or twice heard a distant shout. She shivered. Again it was as it had been with the men and the hounds who had hunted Chole, a fear cloud touching them even this far away.

"They say that man is the most dangerous animal of all, Lorrie. But this night the hunters and not the quarry are the dangerous ones."

"Whom are they hunting?"

"A prisoner escaped from a camp in the North, a beaten man trying to make his way home to ruins and a lost cause."

"Do—do you know him then?" Lorrie asked.

Lotta looked at her in silence for a long moment. "I know what he is, I can guess what made him so. The man himself I do not know."

"But you are going to help him, as you did the others?"

"Perhaps—only perhaps, Lorrie. For I cannot govern the choice of the house. It offers shelter by its own desire, not mine. My people have some powers, Lorrie. We can bend and weave, twist and spin. But there are other arts, equal but apart, and these we cannot influence, though we must abide by their results."

"I don't understand."

Lotta was smiling again. "Not now, Lorrie, not now. But the time will come that you do. If you were not what you are, then the house would never have opened to you even this much. For it chooses its people. A last choice, however, remains yours. Now, I think we shall ride the woods path. For those are very noisy hunters down there, and they must have long since driven any game within hearing into other hiding."

She raised her whip and with it held aside a drooping branch, then turned her mount to the right. Lorrie followed and the branch fell back into place behind them. This was a very narrow way, so narrow they must ride single file, so shut in by trees and bushes that, leafless though those were, they made two walls. Now and then Lotta stopped. In that shadowed place Lorrie could not see what the older girl did, but she thought that she listened.

All at once Lorrie turned her head. Did she really hear a thin, far-off cry? Or— Again she shivered. Lotta was bearing right, where the brush was thinner. They had to ride bent low in the saddles for this was no path, merely a seeking through the woods. At last they came out by a fence made of rails laid crisscross in angles, and Lotta followed this.

Lorrie dropped Bevis' reins and held her hands to her ears with a gasp. That shrill cry was inside her head and it hurt! It was too close, much too close.

She heard Lotta speak a word that had no meaning. The harsh sound ended as if silenced by that word. Again Lotta spoke in a kind of singsong, not as she had the night they had found Chole, but in another way, as if she were calling with a firm intention of being answered.

The snow in the field beyond the fence was unmarked by any trail. But farther along, in one of the fence corners, something stirred. Lorrie could not help being afraid. When she had been in the sleigh that other time she had known the fear broadcast by the hunters, by Chole, but this was something else. It was as if Lotta, so close

Lorrie could almost reach out and touch her, was not there at all, but that Lorrie was alone while something very strange crawled out to meet her.

Now that stirring in the shadows became a man, who pulled himself up to lean heavily against the rails. He did not try to move toward them, but waited for them to come to him.

Lotta did, but Lorrie remained where she was, though she was not too far away to hear Lotta's voice as she leaned forward a little in her saddle to ask:

"Who are you?"

"Who has the Call?" a hoarse voice answered. "Not what you think I am, I am afraid. I was given the Call to use when all else failed me, as this night it has. But any power was not mine, but another's. I do not claim to be more than I am."

"Which is well for you. To make rash claims to such powers—"

"Could not bring me into more danger than I know, lady. Raise your voice a little and those louts beating the river banks will be up to dispose of the problem I am. And at this point I do not believe I care very much any more."

"Can you walk?" To Lorrie, Lotta's voice sounded cold and demanding.

"After a fashion, ma'am. I've run and I've crawled, perhaps there is enough strength left in me to walk—but not far."

The shadow lurched away from the fence, stumbled toward Lotta, caught at her skirt. There was a ripping sound as the man almost went to his knees. Lotta reached down and caught at him.

"Hold to my stirrup!" There was a note of command in her voice. "Lorrie, go back to the road, watch— See that they do not come from the bridge without warning."

Lorrie edged Bevis around in the narrow space between the edge of the wood and the fence. Could she find her way back to the road? She was not at all sure. But Bevis started confidently on and she thought she might leave it to him. That choice proved right, for he went through the trees to that very narrow path. Lorrie listened for any shouting, any sound that the searchers by the river were moving up to the house. She reached the screen of boughs that hid the entrance to its path, and looked down the road.

Torch lights moved together, as if the men who carried them were gathering into a single party. What must she do if they started up toward the house?

"Lorrie?" came a soft call from the path behind her.

"They are gathering together by the bridge," she answered.

"We must cross the road before they come any closer. It is only a little farther, you *must* make it!" Lotta must be talking to the man.

"Tell that to my legs, ma'am. This is a case of the spirit being willing, but the flesh very weak."

"Hang on. Lorrie, move Bevis between us and the bridge as a screen. Do you understand?"

"Yes." Lorrie caught up the branch marking the end of the path. Lotta moved into the open, her horse coming step by cautious step, that dark figure stumbling painfully beside her. Then they were on the road, and Lorrie came to the other side, Bevis matching step to Lotta's horse, so that the stranger staggered between them.

Back they went to Octagon House. When they reached the lane that led to the stable, Lorrie could hear the man breathing in harsh gasps, saw him wavering as if he could hardly stand. Lotta kept a grasp on his shoulder.

"Get Phineas," Lotta ordered. Lorrie broke away, urged Bevis into a leap forward, scrambled out of the saddle by the stable, and ran for the door.

"Phineas!"

He came out in a rush, passing Lorrie as if he did not see her, but ran down the lane to Lotta.

"Here!" He was beside the stranger, pulling at him.

"Lorrie—the horses—into the stable! They are coming!"

Lorrie caught the reins of Lotta's mount as Lotta dismounted and held to the stranger's other side, turning him with Phineas' help to the garden path that led to the back door. She took Lotta's horse and Bevis, pulling them into the stable, shutting the door on them, before she ran back to that slowly moving trio on the walk.

Now she could hear only too clearly the voices on the road. Lotta was right, the hunters were coming.

"Up here!"

"I can't—"

"You must!" That was Lotta.

Somehow he must have found the strength, for they did get him up those four steps, through the door into the back hall.

"Hurry!"

They pulled him on, Lorrie following. Something dropped to the floor as they came into the kitchen and Lorrie caught it up. Chole stood by the table, but at the sight of them she ran and pushed open the door to the back hall, went before them to open the way into the green room, and then to the chamber with the painted floor. Phineas and Lotta lowered the man into the chair and his head fell back against its high back, his beard-matted chin pointing to the ceiling. He was heavily bearded and his eyes were deeply sunken. Under dirty rags his body was very thin and he shivered as if he had not been really warm for a long time. Lotta turned to Phineas.

"Look to the horses!"

"I will that——" And he was gone.

Then she spoke to Chole. "Some soup—and blankets——"

But Chole stood staring at the half-conscious man. Then she looked at Lotta.

"He's—one of *them*."

"So? In this room, in this house, do you question, Chole?"

For a moment they stared at each other, and Lorrie had the feeling that though they made no sound, yet they spoke together in a way she did not understand.

"Would he be *here*," asked Lotta in a less stern voice, "if what you wish to believe was true?"

Slowly Chole shook her head. Then she, too, went.

Now the man in the chair seemed to rouse a little. He moved his feet, and Lorrie saw there were great holes worn in his boot soles. His hands lifted from the arms of the chair and went to the front of his coat, which was tied together with bits of string through holes.

"Where—where——" He opened his eyes and pulled at the front of his coat as if he hunted for something he carried there and now could not find. "Where——"

For the first time Lorrie glanced down at what she held in her hands. It was a very shallow wooden box or tray, about six inches square. Glued within it were shells, a great many small shells, along with shiny seeds. It was a picture, a heart of brown-red seeds surrounded by flowers of shells and, in the middle, spelled out by seeds, two words: "Truly Thine."

"Is this what you want?" Lorrie held it out to him.

His eyes opened wider as he looked at what she held. Then his lips twisted and he made a queer sound.

"We—cling to things," he said. "Too long sometimes. To make something keeps a man alive. Even in the hell camp it kept my mind alive. But—no—not any more. There is no need now." He took the shell-and-seed picture from Lorrie.

With it in his hand, he sat a little straighter in the chair and looked about him, last of all at Lotta. "For what it is still worth in this mad, troubled world," he said, "I am Charles Dupree, at your service, ma'am. And I believe, unless I have totally lost all count of time, that this is something of a feast day." Ragged scarecrow that he was, he leaned forward in a gesture that had the ghost of grace about it. "Perhaps"—he coughed and then smiled at Lotta—"perhaps, I should now say it. Madam, will you be—my valentine?"

Lotta caught the shell picture as it fell from his hand. And he would have gone to the floor if she had not pushed him back in the chair.

"Lorrie—the wall!" She was holding Charles

in the chair. "Press the two ends of the middle shelf, both of them together!"

Lorrie stretched her arms wide, her finger tips just touching the points Lotta indicated. She pressed as hard as she could. Then she jerked back as the wall moved. There was a tiny triangular closet beyond with a very thin slit of window.

Chole stood at the other door. She carried a mug from which a curl of steam rose. And then there was a heavy rapping that echoed through the whole house.

"Them!" Chole flashed across the room and set the mug in the closet, dropped a blanket from her shoulder to the floor, was back again. "Leave him to me, Mis' Lotta. You go an' talk t' *them!*"

Lorrie started forward to help Chole, but she never reached the side of the chair. Light and dark whirled to become moonlight and shadow around the doll house. She turned slowly to face the other wall. There was no opening there. But —she had to know. Slowly she went to the empty shelf where books had stood it seemed only seconds earlier. She put her finger tips and pushed, then moved back. There was no quick outward swing this time, but the shelf wall *had* moved a little. Lorrie put her fingers into the new crack and pulled.

There it was—a bare little three-cornered closet, empty of all except shadows. But it was there. Lorrie pushed the wall back into place. All at once she was cold and the shadows seemed larger and blacker, the moonlight strip thinner and weaker. She wanted real light and real people. So she ran, Sabina streaking before her, back into the house of her own time.

One Golden Needle

"FOR YOU, with all the thank you's from the committee." Lorrie held out the tissue-wrapped package to Miss Ashemeade. "And here is the scrapbook too. The girls were all very careful. We know it is a precious thing. You were kind to talk to Aunt Margaret about our borrowing it."

Miss Ashemeade smiled as she took the package. "If I had not known you would cherish it, Lorrie, I would not have lent it to you. Nothing, child, is too precious to give or lend to one who has need of it, always remember that. And now, let us see what this is."

She drew off the ribbon, put aside the tissue paper, and looked at the offering from the committee.

"It was the prettiest one," Lorrie said. "We all worked on it."

Miss Ashemeade held the valentine up so that the sunlight fell across the lacy paper and the center bouquet of flowers, touched the golden letters Lizabeth had so skillfully cut from the gilt paper in the shape of a twisted rope.

"To Our Valentine," Miss Ashemeade read. "You have done well, all of you, Lorrie. I shall give you a note for the committee. And so these are what you are going to offer for sale at your fair?"

"We made fifty," Lorrie answered with pride. "Oh, they're not all as large as this one. But we tried to copy the ones in the book we liked best. And Mrs. Raymond said they were 'works of art,'" Lorrie quoted.

Miss Ashemeade set the valentine carefully up on top of her embroidery table. Lorrie watched her and then paid more attention to the room. It was different. Now, with a sharp stab of fear, she knew why. The long table was bare, there were no longer any piles of materials and ribbons, any piece of work waiting the repairing needle.

The embroidery frame was empty and put back against the wall. Though there was a fire on the hearth this late Friday afternoon and Sabina lay curled before it, and there were candles lighted, for the first time Lorrie did not feel the old safe welcome. She looked to Miss Ashemeade troubled.

"You aren't cleaning now—" She wanted that to be a question, but it sounded more a statement of a fact she did not want to believe.

"No, Lorrie, the cleaning and the clearing are almost done."

"The house! Miss Ashemeade, that meeting— Couldn't the lawyer do anything to help you? They are not going to tear down Octagon House! They can't!"

She had been so busy with the committee, with end of the term lessons and tests—she had been too busy to care! Maybe—maybe she could have done something— There had been her idea of trying to get people interested in saving the house. If she had only paid attention, tried— The chill within Lorrie spread. She shivered as she looked about the room again and noticed all the familiar things now gone from it. What— what would happen now?

"Lorrie." Miss Ashemeade's quiet voice drew her attention from the room to its mistress. "In this much you are right, the time of Octagon House is fast drawing to a close. But that is the natural course of life, dear child. Nothing remains unchanged, unless it withdraws from life itself. By man's measurement Octagon House has had a long life, well over a hundred years. It has seen many changes around it, and now it shall be changed in turn."

"It will be torn down! Gone—not just changed. It's—it's all wrong!" Lorrie had jumped to her feet and that denial came out of her in a shrill voice.

Miss Ashemeade no longer smiled. She gazed at Lorrie very soberly and intently.

"Lorrie, one cannot say no to life and remain the same. When you first came here, you were trying to say no to change. You thought you could not find anything good in a new way of life, was that not true?"

She paused, and Lorrie tried to remember back to the days before Octagon House opened its doors for her.

"Then the house had something to offer you. It is, and it has always been, a refuge, Lorrie. Do you understand what I mean?"

"A safe place," Lorrie answered.

"A safe place. And some who found their way here, child, were so beaten and hurt by life that this refuge became a home. In this house there is a choice one may make—to re-enter life again, or to stay. You thought you were un-happy and alone. But were you ever as unhappy and frightened and alone as Phebe and Phineas, Chole and Nackie, and Charles Dupree?"

Lorrie did not know quite what Miss Ashe-meade was trying to tell her. "They came— Lotta brought them—because they were being hunted—people after them—"

"They were hunted, yes. Two orphan children,

and two escaped slaves, and a prisoner of war. The house chose to shelter them, and in turn they chose to remain in the house. You thought you were being hunted, too, but what were you running from, Lorrie?"

"Jimmy Purvis—the boys—" Lorrie began slowly, trying to think *why*. Somehow it all seemed so silly now. "And I guess everything else—missing Grandmother and Hampstead, and being lonely. I was silly and stupid"—she felt her face grow hot—"just as they said I was."

"These things seemed big to you then, Lorrie. But how do you find them now?"

"Small," Lorrie admitted.

"Because you have learned that time can change some things?"

Suddenly Lorrie asked a question of her own. "Miss Ashemeade—the doll house—this house —are they the same?" She herself did not know quite what she meant, yet it was important.

Miss Ashemeade shook her head. "That I cannot tell you. It's not that I *will* not, but I truly *cannot*. But know this much: if you had not had the power within you that opened the doors, you would not have seen what you did. The house chooses, it always does. And now that you have seen some things, there is reason to believe that time may open more doors for you, if you wish."

"Miss Ashmeade, if Octagon House must go, where will you and Hallie live?"

Once more Miss Ashemeade smiled. "Dear child, that is a worry no one need have. And now I believe you have one last row on your sampler to finish. Shall we sew for a while?"

She put aside the valentine and opened the top of her table. Lorrie picked up her own workbox and got out the strip of linen with its rows and rows of stitches. A little surprised, she surveyed the record of her learning. Why, it was longer than she had thought, beginning with simple out-line stitching and French knots, and going onto featherstitching, chain stitching, into more com-plicated work.

Miss Ashemeade had taken a small package out of one of the table compartments and was unfolding a strip of cloth.

"Will you set the music box, Lorrie?" she asked.

As the tinkling notes sounded through the quiet of the room, Lorrie was not surprised when Miss Ashemeade began to sing in that unknown other language. But she was not stitching tapestry, or mending lace, or making a collar—

Collar, thought Lorrie in sudden surprise. Miss Ashemeade had made that velvet collar for Sabina for Christmas. But Sabina had not worn it then, nor had Lorrie seen it again since the day it had been fashioned.

What was Miss Ashemeade making now? Lorrie leaned forward a little to see, for it was small. Yes, that was the golden needle flashing,

though there was no sun to light it today. But
—she was making a doll dress!

And as she sewed on, she glanced now and
then to a small picture that had been wrapped
up with the material. By leaning forward just
a little farther Lorrie could see the picture clearly,
and with a start of surprise recognized the lady
in it.

That was Lotta as she had seen her last with
Charles. Only instead of a riding habit she wore
a lovely dress of lace that spread out in rows of
ruffles from her small waist. And Miss Ashemeade was copying that dress, sewing on such
tiny ruffles that Lorrie would not have believed
anyone could make such invisibly small stitches
unless she had watched them in progress. Miss
Ashemeade sang. Again Lorrie found her own
needle moving in time to that singing, with ease
and pleasure in what she was doing.

When her last row of sampler stitches was
completed, she folded the length of material and
placed it neatly in the bottom of her box, beneath the tray that held the needlecase, reels,
and spools. She sat quietly, content to watch
the flashing of the golden needle in and out, and
then she found herself repeating the words of
the song along with Miss Ashemeade, not knowing what they meant, except that they were a
very necessary part of what Miss Ashemeade was
now doing.

How long they sat there Lorrie did not know

or care. For her the warmth and the safe feeling had returned to the room. But at last Miss Ashemeade set a final stitch and cut her thread. The dress was finished. She smoothed it with her fingers and then further unrolled the large square of material. Within lay a second dress of soft rose-pink and with it a ruffled apron.

"Oh!" Lorrie cried in distress. "You broke your needle—the gold needle!"

Miss Ashemeade no longer sang. And as she put down the needle it no longer flashed. It was broken in two, and somehow it no longer seemed gold, but lay in dull pieces, as if the stitching it had just done had drawn out of it all the life it had once held.

"Its work was done, my dear." Miss Ashemeade did not sound sorry. "It was very old and its usefulness was finished."

Lorrie eyed the doll dresses. She wanted to ask why Miss Ashemeade had made them, but somehow she could not. It was as if such a question would have been rude.

Miss Ashemeade put them away, rolled up in the material. She shut down the lid of the sewing table.

"Now, Lorrie, if you will fetch pen and paper. I do want to thank the committee for their charming gift."

As Miss Ashemeade wrote, Lorrie moved to the fireplace. Sabina sat up and began to wash. It was so quiet in the room that the faint scratching of pen on paper could be heard, even the lick-lick of Sabina's rough pink tongue against her black fur. Suddenly Lorrie did not like that quiet. Hallie—where was Hallie? She listened for any noise from the kitchen. But perhaps the walls of the old house were too thick, for if Hallie were busy, no sound could be heard here.

Miss Ashemeade sealed her envelope with a small wafer, and then brought out from some inner pocket of her wide skirt another envelope.

"Lorrie, I am going to ask you to do something that is very important to me. And I shall also ask you not to question it. I believe I can trust you."

"Yes, Miss Ashemeade."

"As you leave here tonight, you will find the key in the lock of the back door. You will lock the door, then you will put the key into this envelope, seal the envelope, and mail it at the corner post box."

"Miss Ashemeade!" Lorrie dared to catch and hold the hand offering her the envelope. "Please, Miss Ashemeade, what are you going to do?"

"I said no questions, Lorrie. And do not be afraid, because there is nothing to fear, that I promise you. I told you once that belief was needful. Believe me now."

Lorrie took the envelope. "I do."

"And now, Lorrie, it grows late."

But Lorrie did not turn at once to the door. "Please—I *will* see you again?"

Miss Ashemeade smiled. Sabina came running lightly across the room and jumped into her lap.

"I believe you will, Lorrie. Remember, belief is very important—belief and the need for seeing with the heart as well as with the eyes. Always remember that. And now, goodbye for a little while, Lorrie."

"Goodbye." Lorrie could linger no longer after that dismissal, but somehow she was almost afraid to go, afraid that if she went out of this room she would never see it again. She turned as she reached the door to look back for the last time.

Sabina lay at ease across her mistress' lap and Miss Ashemeade was stroking her. The shadows were gathering darker and darker in the far corners of the room, beginning to creep out toward its center.

"Please, may I say goodbye to Hallie too?" Lorrie asked.

"Of course, my dear, if you can find her."

Lorrie closed the door and crossed the hall to the kitchen. The door was shut and did not open to her pull. What had Miss Ashemeade once said, on her first exploration of the house—go anywhere the doors will open. This one would not.

Lorrie rapped on it, but there was no answer. But she must say goodbye to Hallie! Somehow, tonight especially, that was important. With her knuckles still resting against the stubbornly closed panels, Lorrie called:

"Goodbye, Hallie, goodbye!"

Still that did not seem enough. Alarmed, why she was not quite sure, Lorrie turned to the door through which she had come only moments earlier. She would ask Miss Ashemeade. But that door could not now be opened either. She lifted her hand though she did not knock. After her last goodbye, Lorrie somehow felt she must not disturb the mistress of Octagon House again.

She put on her wraps and boots. The key was in the lock, just as Miss Ashemeade had said it would be. She let herself out, then turned the key. For a long moment she stood on the top step, holding it in her hand. She had locked Miss Ashemeade and Hallie inside—why? The key was big and old and heavy. But perhaps they had another key. Maybe Hallie was tired and had gone to rest, and Miss Ashemeade wanted to spare her having to come and lock up.

But then why put the key in an envelope and mail it? Lorrie turned the envelope over in her hand. There were papers inside to make it fat. She dropped the key in quickly and licked the flap shut. The name and address on it—it was meant to go to a Mr. Ernest Thruston—the lawyer!

Belief was important, Miss Ashemeade had said—and don't ask questions. But questions buzzed in Lorrie's head as she walked to the mailbox and dropped in the heavy letter.

Lorrie continued to think about that key and the big envelope while she got supper for Aunt Margaret, who would be late tonight. She kept remembering things that made her more and more uneasy, just why she was not sure. Miss Ashemeade's precious golden needle, dull and broken. And the locked door when she left— Miss Ashemeade certainly could not have risen and walked across the room all by herself to lock the door of the red room in the short time Lorrie had been at the kitchen door! Then who had? Hallie, coming around the other way through the unused parlor?

But always her thoughts came back to the key and why Miss Ashemeade had wanted her to mail it to Mr. Thruston.

Where *would* Miss Ashemeade, Hallie, and Sabina go? Lorrie could not think of them living anywhere else than in Octagon House— they did not belong to the world outside its doors. And what would happen to all the treasures? Would Miss Ashemeade be able to take them with her?

Lorrie glanced about the very small kitchen of the apartment. Imagine Hallie trying to work here! Her beloved stove could not fit in. Suddenly Lorrie wanted to race back through the dusk, knock on the back door—that locked back door—and find Hallie, and the red room, and

Miss Ashemeade just the same as they had been through all the months she had known them. Months, wondered Lorrie. Yes, part of October, all of November, and December, and January, and one week in February—But it seemed to her now that she had been a visitor to Octagon House for far longer than that.

What would become of Bevis and the doll house? Or—for the first time Lorrie's thoughts winged in another direction—*was* there now a Bevis and a doll house? Had there ever been at all?

But Miss Ashemeade knew about Phebe and Phineas, Chole and Nackie, and Charles Dupree. She had said this afternoon that they had chosen to remain in its safety. Did that mean they lived there forever and ever? Lorrie looked at the clock and at the coffeepot put on to perk. Believe, Miss Ashemeade had said.

Lorrie drew a deep breath and stood still. She was staring at the wall but not seeing the brightly polished copper molds hung there to brighten up the dark corner beyond the dinette. There was a new warm feeling inside her. Now—now she believed that Miss Ashemeade, and Hallie, and Sabina were safe too. No matter what would happen to Octagon House, they would be safe—forever!

"Lorrie?" She had not heard Aunt Margaret's key in the door. Now she turned, startled.

Aunt Margaret still had on her coat and hat.

She looked unhappy. "Lorrie, I am so sorry—"

"Sorry for what?" Lorrie was jolted out of her own thoughts.

"About Octagon House." Aunt Margaret had the evening paper in one hand. "The thruway—" She hesitated.

"I know. Miss Ashemeade told me."

"Those poor old ladies. Something must be done for them. Wherever will they go? Lorrie, I think I had better go up there this evening and see if there is any way I may help."

"Miss Ashemeade said they would be safe."

"Safe? Oh, yes, you were there this afternoon. But maybe she did not really understand, Lorrie. The Commissioners announced today that the appeal failed. All those who objected will have to move. Miss Ashemeade is very old, Chick. And sometimes old people do not understand how things can be taken this way by the city."

"She does know, Aunt Margaret. She told me there was no place for Octagon House now."

Aunt Margaret slipped out of her coat. "But there should be!" she said almost fiercely. "We must see what can be done! At least for those poor old ladies."

"Aunt Margaret," Lorrie asked slowly, "do you really think they are poor old ladies?"

Aunt Margaret looked at Lorrie in surprise. Then her expression became thoughtful.

"No, you are right, Lorrie. Miss Ashemeade may be old, but I do not believe that she would allow anyone to make decisions for her. And she told you she has plans?"

"Yes and—" Lorrie told her about the key and the letter.

"Lock the back door behind you and mail the key—and you did it? But, Lorrie, leaving the two of them locked in and— Why, whyever would they want that? Lorrie, you stay right here—understand?"

Aunt Margaret pulled on her coat, ran out into the hall, and was gone, not quite shutting the door behind her. For a moment Lorrie's amazement was part fear. And then the certainty of moments earlier returned to reassure her, and she knew there was no need to worry about Miss Ashemeade and the other inhabitants of Octagon House. She went on with supper preparations, listening for Aunt Margaret's return.

And return she did before not many minutes had passed. There was an odd expression on her face as she came once more into the kitchen.

"I don't know why," she said. "I got as far as the gate and then, why, then, Lorrie, I just knew it was all right with them."

Lorrie noded. "I know it too."

But Aunt Margaret still had that strange look on her face, as if right before her eyes something had happened that she could not believe, even though she saw it happen. Then she shook her head.

The letter came the following Friday. But as

that was the day of the fair, they did not open it until late. Aunt Margaret had come to the P.T.A. supper, and she and Lorrie did not get back home until after nine. The envelope was waiting in their mailbox, a long white one with a business address in the upper corner and it was addressed to them both: Miss Margaret Gerson, Miss Lorrie Mallard.

Aunt Margaret, very puzzled, read it aloud. They were to go to Octagon House on Saturday morning at eleven, and it was signed Ernest Thruston.

"Miss Ashemeade's lawyer," Lorrie explained.

"But why?" Aunt Margaret read it through a second time, this time to herself. "I can't understand— Well, it sets one's imagination to working, doesn't it? Luckily I am free tomorrow."

It was snowing a little when they opened the front gate of Octagon House the next day. Again the proud deer had a small ridge of white down his back as he stared over their heads. Lorrie looked at him a little sadly and hoped he would find another home when they took away his lawn and garden.

There were tracks in the snow on the walk, as if someone had gone around the house not too long before, and they followed those to the same back door they had always used. Aunt Margaret rapped and the door was opened, not by a smiling Hallie, but by a man who said at once and a little sharply:

"Miss Gerson?"

"Yes, and Lorrie."

He brought them into the red room. But Lorrie shivered. There was no fire on the hearth. A lamp and some candles had been lighted, but all the warmth and cheer had gone out of the room. The tall back chair was empty. Aunt Margaret asked the question that Lorrie could not voice.

"Miss Ashemeade?"

"She has gone. Of course, she has always been a will unto herself. The key and her instructions were mailed to me. Brrr—these old houses without central heating—nothing but damp and cold! If you don't mind." He glanced about him as if he did not care for the room or the house, and would like to be away as soon as possible. "Miss Ashemeade has made certain dispositions of her property that I am empowered to carry out. Your niece, Lorrie Mallard, is to have the contents of the toy room. If you will please come with me."

"The toy room?" echoed Aunt Margaret. "But—"

It was a strange house, Lorrie thought as they went from shrouded parlor to bedroom, where now covers were also draped all over the furniture. Then Mr. Thruston pushed open the last door and they were in the room with the painted floor.

There were Bevis and the house, just as they had always been.

"Why, Lorrie! A doll house, and a rocking horse—" Aunt Margaret stared at those. But there was more in the room now, Lorrie noted. The box from which Miss Ashemeade had unpacked the wonderful Christmas ornaments stood to one side and on it rested both the workbox she had used and the scrapbook of valentines.

Aunt Margaret walked slowly around the house, peering into its windows.

"This—this is a museum piece, Mr. Thruston. And—and we do not have room for it in the apartment."

"I believe Miss Ashemeade foresaw that problem, Miss Gerson." Mr. Thruston held a piece of paper. "It has been arranged that most of the furnishings of this house, having historical value, be presented to the Ashton Historical Society. The doll house and the horse may be placed on loan with them also, a loan that may be terminated upon demand at any time by your niece. They will have safekeeping, and they will doubtless be enjoyed by the public—I believe the school classes make yearly visits to the Society. But whenever she wishes, she may reclaim them. And now, I dislike hurrying you, Miss Gerson, but there are certain articles left to *your* care. If you will just come and see—"

"That wonderful house— Yes, I'll come," answered Aunt Margaret.

Lorrie waited until they had left and then she stepped around to the side of the house where the dining room was—the room Miss Ashemeade had made so much her own. In spite of the gloom in the room, she had caught a glimpse, a glinting sparkle against the base. Now she knelt on the floor to see it better. Yes, she was right! There was a gold chain, and strung on it seven small keys, while an eighth stood in the keyhole of the drawer.

She turned that key and drew open the drawer. It was one of the wider ones.

"Lotta." She did not need to touch the beautiful lace dress she had seen Miss Ashemeade make, nor the doll who wore it. "Hallie." No longer bent and old, but young as Miss Lotta—wearing the rosy dress. "Sabina." Small, quiet, with her silver-belled collar. "Hello." Lorrie bent closer to whisper. "Now—all of you—wait for me."

Softly she shut the drawer and turned the key in its lock. Why had she said that? Wait for her —how?—where? Until someday when she had a house big enough to hold the doll house? When again there might be a chance to visit it, meet again those who would live there for always and always?

One, two, three, four drawers with their occupants. What lay in the other four?

She tried a key in the next and opened it— nothing. Then a second and third—they were empty. But when she pulled out the fourth—Lorrie looked closer. It was the wooden needle box. She picked it up and opened it. One golden needle was left, thrust firmly into the velvet. Lorrie did not touch it, but put the box back and locked the drawer.

Then she tried them all. They were safely locked. The house, yes, let them put the house in the museum where anyone who wished might look in it. But the people of the house—let them be as safe as they had chosen to be.

Lorrie dropped the chain with its keys into her workbox, and took that up with the scrapbook. She could get the ornament box later. Holding the box and the book, she went to Bevis and stroked his arching neck. Thump, thump, he rocked back and forth, but he did not change. Lorrie was not disappointed. That was as it should be —for now.

She went to the door and then looked back at the waiting house, at Bevis. Wait they would, house and horse, as long or as short—as time.

"Goodbye," said Lorrie very softly, "for a while. Goodbye—"

The floor creaked. Had or had not Bevis rocked to nod her an approving answer?

ABOUT THE AUTHOR
AND ILLUSTRATOR

ANDRE NORTON was born in Cleveland and attended Western Reserve University. For many years, she worked as a children's librarian in the Cleveland Public Library. Miss Norton started her writing career as an editor of the literary page on her high school paper and published her first book before the age of twenty-one. She has written close to ninety books with millions of copies in print. In 1977, she received the Gandalf Award for her life's work in fantasy at the annual World Science Fiction Convention. FUR MAGIC, OCTAGON MAGIC, STAR KA'AT, and STAR KA'AT WORLD, by Andre Norton, are published in Archway Paperback editions.

MAC CONNER was born in Newport, New Jersey and graduated from Pennsylvania Museum School of Art in Philadelphia and Grand Central School of Art in New York City. He is an illustrator of both books and magazines. Mr. Conner and his wife live in Sussex, New Jersey.